Passion Rising

JA *Huss*
Johnathan McClain

Julie & Johnathan

HUSSMCCLAIN.COM

Edited by RJ Locksley
Cover Design by JA Huss

PASSION RISING

JA HUSS & JOHNATHAN McCLAIN

CHAPTER ONE

MADDIE & TYLER

DECEMBER 27TH
Four Days Until New Year's Eve

MADDIE

"You reach the spaceship jail and find a woman behind bars—"

"If her name is Maddie, then I fuck her," Tyler says, his hands on my hips, rocking my body back and forth, trying to make me fuck him harder.

"That's not an option." I laugh, looking down at him over the top of the yellowed paperback book I'm holding in my hand. "Stop jumping ahead. It's cheating. You're not taking this seriously."

He just grins at me like a mischievous child. "Oh, I'm sorry. I'm not taking *Choose Your Own Sex Adventure* seriously enough. My bad."

We found a box of old paperbacks in the closet of the room Tyler's been living in at Robert and Evan's house. They're like vintage nineteen seventies porn books, but you get to choose different options as you go through the story. Like... *His cock is hard and throbbing, do you suck it? (Go to page 31.) Or do you give him a hand job? (Go to page 43.)*

It's been barely forty-eight hours since all the shit that went down in Mexico...went down. And we've avoided talking about it. To anyone else or to each other.

It's actually pretty easy not to talk about it with anyone else. The only person we told is Evan. And in true Evan fashion, he seemed fairly non-plussed. Tyler told him everything, he listened, and then finally just said, "Well that's fucking crazy. Let's eat." And that was it. We had dinner after that. Tyler thinks Evan's disappointed that he didn't get to come on the "mission" too.

Both of them are insane.

The whole point of him spending these past couple days in bed was to recover from the beating Logan inflicted on his ribs while we were in Carlos' compound, but he refused to stay in bed unless I stayed with him.

Which is why we're fucking right now. Apparently, taking it easy isn't something Tyler Morgan does. So I came up with this book idea to make him go slow.

Not that it's working, but it's definitely fun.

"You have to let me finish the scenario before you answer."

"Whose rules are these anyway?" He grabs the paperback from my hand and tosses it across the room. It hits the wall with a thud and falls to the floor. "Let's make our own scenario. I'll go first. You're on the planet Brown Chicken Brown Cow—"

I laugh. Because it comes out *bow-chica-bow-wow.*

"—which plays a Barry White soundtrack twenty-four seven..."

"You're dumb." I giggle.

"And the first thing you see when you exit your spaceship—where you've been in hibernation for a thousand years—"

"Wait, am I old?"

"Nah," Tyler says. "You were in cryogenic hibernation. In fact, you're sexy as fuck. Sexier than ever. Like… your hair is perfect. Blowing in the soft, hot Brown Chicken Brown Cow wind—"

"Jesus Christ," I say.

"So you're basically sex-starved, OK?"

"Got it." I laugh.

"And the first thing you see is a naked man with a huge Chuckie Stiff."

I close my eyes and shake my head.

"Do you subdue him with your feminine wiles and make him fuck you against a wall—"

"That's a no," I say. "He's got broken ribs!"

"Bruised," Tyler corrects me. "Ain't nothin' broken, babe. Or do you drop to your knees, take his big cock in your mouth, and make him come in your throat?"

I stare down at him, trying not to grin. "Those are my two choices?"

"Only two ya got." He winks.

I lift myself up, letting his hard cock slip out from my pussy. Tyler's face lights up with glee as I ease myself down his stomach, kissing him lightly as I descend, my eyes glued to his.

His hand automatically goes to my head. His fingertips thread into my hair and grab it, urging me on.

"If I make you come in my throat," I say, my words husky and thick, "then the adventure is over, I get out of bed and go make us lunch while you stay here… alone. So are you sure those are my only two options?"

"Shit," he says. "OK, I didn't think this through. One sec…" He thinks for a moment, that one eyebrow lifted, and says, "OK, new scenario. You're still sex-starved, still looking hot as fuck, and still on Brown Chicken Brown Cow."

"Got it."

"Do you lick his balls and finger his ass—"

I laugh so loud, I think Robert and Evan can hear me from the living room.

Tyler waggles his eyebrows. "God, I hope you choose that one."

"Just give me the other option, pervert."

"Or do you get back on your spaceship and take a vow of celibacy?"

Clever, clever Tyler Morgan. "OK, Mr. I've-got-her-right-where-I-want-her… Ball-licking and ass-sticking it is."

"Fuckin' sweet," he says, doing a fist pump in the air.

I ease myself down farther, my tongue doing a little swirly dance across his bare stomach, my teeth nipping at the happy trail of hair leading to the Promised Land. I take his hard cock in my hand, wrapping my fingers around his wide girth, and squeeze gently.

"Fuck yeah," Tyler says. "Squeeze harder."

I do, because it turns me on to realize my hands are barely big enough to encircle him. Plus, I like it when he closes his eyes, and this makes him do that now. I put his cock right up to my face, my tongue slipping across the tip of his head, even though that wasn't in the prescribed scenario.

Tyler makes a little grunting sound, which I love, and then I put my mouth on his shaft and lick him as I descend to his base. His balls are hard and tight when I cup them and this makes him open his legs a little in expectation. I finger the soft skin between his ass and his cock, stroking it gently.

Tyler fists my hair harder in response and murmurs something encouraging, but incoherent, so I keep going, my tongue flicking across his balls before I place my whole mouth on them and suck.

"Jesus," he says.

That's when my finger finds his asshole and presses into the tight muscles. He sucks in a breath, holds it, and then releases it, his cock jumping in my hand as I continue to suck his balls until one of them is entirely inside my mouth.

He's moaning now, which is my cue to stop and hold still.

After a few seconds he opens one eye. "What?"

"Next scenario," I say. "Ready?" I grin at him mischievously.

"Hit me with it. Quick."

"OK," I say. "The Ageless Space Goddess is between your legs, her breath tickling the soft skin of your balls, her finger on your asshole." I wiggle my finger a little to keep him in the moment.

"Yeah," he says. "And?"

"Does she rim you with her tongue—"

He smiles so big I almost lose it.

"Or does she turn around and let you lick her pussy *while* she rims you with her tongue?"

Now it's his turn to laugh loudly. Robert and Evan heard that for sure.

"Option B," he says, clapping his hands and sitting up a little to brace himself against the headboard.

"Your wish, Commander Morgan, is my command."

TYLER

"Option B, Option B, Option B!" I say it like Eddie Murphy in *The Nutty Professor*. *"Hercules, Hercules, Hercules."*

As I'm pushing my neck back to get the angle I want that will allow me to maximize my space thrust, I can still feel the twinge of pain in my abs. I don't want to let Maddie know that it stings. She couldn't believe that the x-rays she made me get showed no breaks. I tried to tell her. Ain't no weak-ass Logan and his weak-ass bat gonna break anything on Tyler Morgan!

It's definitely still tender. But you know what? I'm alive. And Maddie's alive. And even if my friggin' spine was snapped in half, I'd still find a way to have naked time with her. Because suffering is temporary. Maddie, naked, by my side—shit, that's the reason I'll be waking up every morning for the rest of my life.

She pivots a hundred and eighty degrees, and now I'm looking at her exquisite ass. Putting my hands on her cheeks, I let the rough, gnarled skin of my palms brush over the satiny perfection of hers. I massage her, getting off on the sound of her purring and moaning as I knead her flesh and let my thumbs slide along the crease of her backside and down into the slippery wet folds between her legs. As I touch her, her head falls forward and she wraps her mouth around my cock again. I automatically thrust my hips up in response and she bobs her head, bringing up her hand to simultaneously stroke the base.

Then she pulls her head up, twists her neck to look at me, and says, "Sorry. Detour. It was necessary."

"Shit. Yeah. It seemed pretty necessary. Carry on."

She smiles and turns her head back around. Taking her hips and pulling her back toward my mouth, I simultaneously lift my legs as she presses herself forward, her breasts blanketing my cock and imprisoning it in between the soft, velvety skin of her chest and my rugged and marred lower abs. Contorting my legs back so that her tongue can have unfettered access to my asshole definitely causes me to feel a pinch in my ribcage. She must sense it because she asks, "Does this hurt?"

"Fuck, no, it doesn't hurt. Get busy, Ageless Space Goddess. There are uncharted universes to explore."

"Babe—" she starts to semi-protest again. But she stops talking the second I wrap my hands around her thighs and bury my face inside her.

"Oh, my God," she says on a tiny, astonished laugh. It's like she forgets what it feels like to have my mouth on her pussy in between the times that it's there. That's cool. I have no problem reminding her.

And now it's my turn to express astonishment. "Oh, fuck," I say with a particular and new yearning as her hot breath heralds the arrival of her tongue darting into my ass. Her tits rubbing on my aching cock and her stomach resting on my aching ribs are glorious agony. I'm cloaked in her sensuality. But all that is being upstaged by the feeling of her tongue striking my asshole like a velvet dagger.

Pressing down on her ass hard so that she can't accidentally knee me in my still-healing side, I force my own tongue deeper into the opening between her legs. She shudders and trembles as I let my tongue unfold to its maximum length, very nearly ripping it out of the back of my throat as it laps at her tender, pink flesh, and I drink in

11

all the wetness flowing from inside. I feel so goddamn happy right now, I almost want to sing. And so I do.

I pull my tongue back, letting it dance tiny circles on her clit, and I start humming as my mouth wraps itself around her mound of smooth, shaved skin. It's my version of Tibetan throat singing. Deep and guttural and vibratory in a way I know that she can feel throughout her whole body. Her knees are tightening against my sides, and I have to use more force to press them away, which just causes her to push against me harder, and now we are in an erotic tug of war as I eat her out, she rims me, and I keep humming my indecent melody. Suddenly she stops her licking and I can feel her spit dripping down my ass. We are so tangled up in each other that we are the same person.

"Is that..? Are you humming the theme from *Star Wars?*" she asks.

"Mm-hmm," I acknowledge, still refusing to remove my mouth from her body.

And she bursts out laughing. I love her laugh so much, but right now, in this moment, the bouncing of her ribs against mine as she giggles is a little more than I can handle, so I stop playing around and get back to work.

I take her again with my whole mouth, letting my thumb slip into her asshole with one hand and slapping her ass cheeks hard with the other. She squeals and moans, and even though I can't see her face, I just know that her eyes have rolled back into her head. On a gasping moan— or a moaning gasp, I can't tell which—her head collapses forward again, and she starts licking at my balls and then traces her way back down to *my* asshole. My calves tighten and my ankles begin to shake as she darts her tongue in and out. In and out. And around and around and around.

And quid pro tongue-lash, I decide. Because whatever she does with her mouth to me, I mimic with my lips, and teeth, and tongue on her. If her tongue stabs, mine stabs at her. If she makes tiny circles, I frantically whip my tongue around her clit. If she spits down onto me, I spit up into her.

We are the mirrors of our own perversion.

And when she pulls her head back, gasping for breath, I ask, "Do you need to stop?" I don't want to, but if she needs a breather, I will take the chance to, I dunno, grab an ice pack or some shit. But she doesn't answer. Or she does, just not with words. She slides her hips back, pushing her pussy harder into my mouth, and yanks my cock out from between her tits so she can shove it into her mouth once again.

That lets me drop my legs forward so that they're hanging off the bed, and she hooks her hands under my knees and is now bobbing her head up and down on my dick, double-time.

Dirty cheating little Ageless fuckin' Space Goddess. She wants to make me come first. Yeah. Well.

We'll see about that.

MADDIE

I know he's hurting. I also know he's never gonna admit he's hurting. My only option is to give him everything he wants so he can rest properly. It's practically my duty.

Which makes me giggle.

Tyler pauses, his large hand spread across the cheeks of my ass. Squeezing them, he says, "Something funny?"

Is something funny? Everything's funny with Tyler. Or maybe it's just everything's fun with Tyler. I mean I love his long, fat cock, but I love his sense of humor too. Who hums the theme of Star Wars into a woman's pussy?

That thought only makes me laugh harder, which makes Tyler suck in a breath of air. Shit, I'm really hurting him.

I pull my head up, saliva spilling out from between my lips and dripping onto his cock. "I just... love you, ya know." I take the opportunity to use my spit as lubrication so I can pump him harder.

"How much do you love me?" Tyler asks, his finger caressing the soft skin around my asshole.

"Enough to play Hot Commander Meets the Space Goddess just to keep you in bed," I say, peeking at him over my shoulder. "I'd do anything for you, ya know that, right?"

He gets this sappy look on his face. Like life is good and can't get any better. He's sentimental, that's something I've figured out over the past few weeks. Tyler Morgan is equal parts caring and cold. He is both soft and hard. He can be weak and strong in the same breath depending on circumstance. Fuck with him or the people he loves and he will take you out by any means necessary. But if one of those people he loves asks for a favor... he'd do it. No matter what, he'd do it.

"Anything?" Tyler asks, both eyebrows lifted high on his forehead.

I ease my lips back down over the tip of his cock and murmur, "Anything," as I lower my head and take him fully into my mouth.

I feel him sigh. "Your commander requires more convincing if you want him to save you from eternal celibacy, Goddess." He whispers it right up against my pussy, making the loose folds of skin vibrate.

I close my eyes and think only of the moment. I appreciate that we are alive. That we're together. That the bad stuff is finally behind us.

His tongue swirls against my pussy, alternating between light and forceful probing as I take him deeper into my mouth, until the tip of his head touches the back of my throat. I press my lips tightly against his shaft. I hold him there and enjoy the way his cock fills me up, closing my eyes and flattening my tongue against him. And just when I think I will pass out, or gag, or die from satisfaction—I lift up, saliva spilling out of my mouth once again. Coating his cock as I kiss the tip of his head.

I kiss it over and over and over again. Little fluttery kisses made sloppy from the blow job.

"Turn around," he says.

I close my eyes. Exhale. And then carefully reposition myself so I'm straddling his hips. He's sitting up just enough for me to brace my hands on the headboard and not put pressure on his ribs. Bruised or broken—doesn't matter. He's hurt and the only thing I care about right now is making him feel good.

His cock is peeking out from between my legs. Long and thick, it stretches up over his lower abdomen, reaching for his navel. I rub my pussy against it, letting my lips fold over him as I slowly move back and forth.

Tyler closes his eyes as he smiles. "Fuck. You're trying to kill me."

"No," I say, leaning my head down to kiss his mouth. He tastes like me. "I'm here to save you."

I don't know why I say it, except... I mean it. So I do know why. He said that back when we were still figuring things out. I was his salvation. And I didn't want to accept the job, but that was then, and this is now, and I want nothing more than to be the angel he thinks I am.

So I lift my hips up, take his cock in my hand like it's a precious artifact one needs to respect and be gentle with, and place him at the entrance to my pussy.

His eyes are open again, staring at me in a way that makes my heart melt with love as I lower myself, letting him press up inside me until I am full and complete.

The jokes are in the past now. We're as serious as two people can be. I take my hands off the headboard and place them on his face. His hands find my hips and we stare at each other as we move. Slowly this time. Not rushed or frantic, but carefully. Tenderly. Our bodies joined together—fitting together—like lost puzzle pieces that found their way back into the big picture called happiness.

TYLER

It's all happened so fast. Except it hasn't at all. It's been coming for a lifetime. I didn't know it. She did. And now here we are. The warm desert nights have turned into chilly desert nights, and surprisingly, I find someone who loves me and who I love back, and together we will keep each other warm.

Ain't that a kick in the nuts?

"Thank you," I say.

She makes a face with a furrowed brow and a confused smile and says, "For what? You usually wait until we're done for that."

"Yeah, I know," I tell her, as she keeps moving slowly, agonizingly, erotically back and forth along the length of my cock. "But that's not what I'm thanking you for."

She slows her movement, tilts her head, strokes my hair, and asks, "Then what?"

I take her face in my hands now and lock onto her with an earnestness that you can't fake. "For loving me. For choosing to let go of the anger you had. And for... seeing me. I guess."

She gets a little teary. That's one thing about being a wiseass all the time. When you get serious about some shit, people take notice.

"I never stopped thinking about you," she says. "If I had forgotten you, that'd be one thing. The opposite of love isn't hate, it's ambivalence. I've never been ambivalent about you. Ever." She smiles an aching, yearning, sheepishly precious smile, then says, "I fucking *hated* you."

I laugh, she laughs, even though the tears are still there, and she starts moving again, kissing me hard. Arching my back stings, so I just rotate my hips in circles while she slides back and forth. We're a human gyroscope.

We're trying to be gentle. To be slow. But our need for each other is too great. We've been through more in the last two months than most people endure in a lifetime and we're still here and still able to tell the tale. Not that we will. But it creates an even more brutal urgency to our actions with each other than would normally be there for two people newly in love. Because both of us have been taught the same lesson over, and over, and over again.

Don't take this life too much for granted. It can be taken away when you're least expecting it.

We climax at the same time. She moans and whines and yells. I make a sound that can only be described as "caveman-esque," and then she collapses forward, as is her wont, and I try to pretend that it isn't crushing me. Because... eh. So what?

"Commander Morgan," she gasps, her face buried in my shoulder. "Thanks for saving me from eternal celibacy. Because that was way fucking better."

"Yeah. Celibacy's some bullshit. Fuck you, celibacy."

She laughs at that and that rising and falling of her ribs on mine is a bitch, all right. So, when the laughter dies down, I should just let it rest. Let her be. Let us sit in the moment and not tip any apple carts or whatever.

I *should*, but I've met myself, so I'm not surprised when I say, "I have three different jokes that involve the word 'Uranus.' You want one or all three?"

And her literal bone-shaking laughter starts again.

I'm in the kitchen grabbing a Perrier (which I didn't know I loved as much as I do – those bubbles are delightful) when Evan walks in, dressed in a top coat and carrying just about the most beautiful leather duffel bag I've ever seen. It's brown with this unreal patina on it, and looks as soft as...well, really soft fuckin' leather, I guess. I don't normally notice shit like that but living here must be rubbing off on me. I don't mind. I'm into the idea of becoming a little more sophisticated. I'm gonna be turning over all my old leaves in this upcoming new year, so add sophisticated gentle-person to the list.

As I'm thinking this, a mighty belch, spawned by the Perrier, leaves my lips and I adjust my dick inside the boxer shorts that are the only thing I have on, since

18

Maddie's still naked in bed and I may see if we can go again in a few minutes.

Becoming new-look Tyler Morgan is a process.

"Where you going?" I ask.

"Um, we're heading to Paris for the New Year."

"Oh, shit, really? I didn't know that. When did you plan that?"

"Uh," he says, pausing like he's embarrassed or something. "About forty-five minutes ago? Robert just decided that he wants to get out of town."

That hangs there for a second as he looks at me with those impenetrable black eyes, nodding his head a little bit. I nod too as I take another sip of my water, and then all of a sudden I realize...

"It's because we're fucking too loud, isn't it?"

"Little bit, maybe, yeah."

He answers before I even get the whole question out.

"Shit, dude, I'm sorry," I say. "We're just—"

He puts his hand up to stop me. "Seriously, all good. I've got the time off coming to me, I've been wanting to go somewhere anyway, he's always working... It's cool. You've done me a mitzvah."

I make the sign of the cross at him.

"Catholic, not Jewish, but whatever, the thought is appreciated," he says. "Also, you guys could use the privacy. You've fucking earned it." He pats me on the arm and rubs my shoulder. "You OK, by the way?"

"Yeah, I'm all good. My ribs still hurt a little more than I'm used to, but I did get punched, beaten repeatedly with a bat, run through fire, and blah, blah, blah, so to be expected. I guess."

"Uh-huh. Uh-huh," he says, nodding again. "And how's this?" He taps me on the temple with his index finger.

I kind of stroke my beard absently while thinking about my answer. There's a reason you see people make that gesture when they want to imply that they're thinking. It's an easy habit to fall into. "Honestly, man?" I say. "Better than it's been in a long time. I know that probably sounds fucking nuts, ironically, but... I was even thinking about calling Dr. Eldridge to tell her that I'm cured."

"Yeah. Do that. Shrinks love it when their patients profess their conclusive sanity."

I roll my eyes at him. Not really because I feel the need to, but because it's just kind of our bit. I like to play my role as the scolded best friend properly.

"Um," he says again.

"Yeeeessss?" I ask.

"There is one other thing. I wasn't going to say anything, but..."

I'm getting worried all of a sudden. Evan isn't usually a 'I wasn't going to say anything' kind of a guy.

"What?" I ask. "What is it? What's up?"

"Um, I was at the station three days ago, on Christmas Eve..."

Jesus. Was Christmas Eve only three days ago? Feels like a fucking eon.

"...and, uh, Jack dropped by."

"Jack? Who's Jack? Jack who?" And then I realize Jack who. "Jack my fucking dad, Jack?" He nods. I take a second. My jaw just got really tight. I need to unhinge it. I roll my neck from side to side and it cracks. Violently.

"Jesus. You need a chiropractor?"

"Probably. What did dear old Jack want?"

20

He shrugs. "Dunno. Came by. Told me that he had seen you. Asked if I knew that you were back in town."

"And what'd you say?"

"Nothing, man. Come on. I told him that I knew you were here but that's it."

"You didn't tell him about—"

"Dude. Give me some credit. I didn't tell him anything."

I nod, slowly. Take another sip of my delicious bubble water. "And so what happened?"

"Nothin'. I stared at him a while until he got uncomfortable, and then he split."

I breathe in through my nose, filling my lungs with oxygen, then letting it out the same way. I tap out a tiny rhythmic beat on the countertop while I think about nothing in particular, or at least nothing I can identify. "OK. Thanks. Hey! Have a good trip, bro!" I put the bottle down and go to give him a hug. I do a quick check-in to make sure I'm not still rocking a partial. Not because I give a shit if he feels Chuckie or whatever. I've known the guy my whole life. If you can't press your fat hard-on into your gay best friend's thigh, then what kind of friendship is it really?

No, it's because that cashmere top coat he's wearing must cost at least thirty large, and I don't want to accidentally get post-sex come-drizzle on it. Because I am thoughtful and considerate. New-look Tyler Morgan is a classy motherfucker.

"Love you, man," I tell him as we hug and pat each other on the back.

"Love you too, bro," he says.

Pulling back, I add, "And thank you for, you know, everything."

He smiles and laughs a wee laugh. "Bro isn't just a term of affection. Any time, anywhere. You know this."

I smile a tight grin myself. "Ditto, kiddo." And then... "Oh. Um, does that extend to the Tesla too?" Maddie's car was lost on Halloween and mine was burned the fuck up on Christmas Eve, so I need something to drive. I suppose I could just go buy another one, but if there's a perfectly good all-electric vehicle sitting here, I should do the right thing by the environment. New-look Tyler Morgan is a straight-up conservationist.

"Of, course, man," he says with a weary smile. "Try not to lose it or blow it up."

"It wouldn't blow. It would just burn," I correct him. "There's no fuel anyway."

He sighs and nods his head. Then he turns and heads for the front door. Just as he's got his hand on the doorknob, I call to him, "Hey, Ev?"

"Yep?"

"Have a safe New Year, bro."

He smiles one last time in the open doorway and says, "You too, Ty. Peace."

CHAPTER TWO

MADDIE

I pull up to Annie's house—wait. I guess it's not Annie's house anymore, is it? It's my house. Or no. Because I don't really think I live here. Do I?

I laugh kinda loud as I turn Evan's Tesla off in the driveway. I mean, of course this is my place. I've lived here for almost six months. But now that Annie's gone and Tyler and I are together...

I get out and go inside. There's music coming from the back yard and I can see Caroline and Diane sitting under the old palapa wearing sunglasses. Diane is swirling a pink umbrella around inside her fruity pink drink, while Caroline talks and stabs a toothpick into some red grapes on the plate in front of her.

I open the sliding door and exit the house. "Hey," I say, closing the door behind me. It's not really cold outside, but it's not exactly warm either, so it's curious that they're out here. But then again, not really. They spend a lot of time outside when they're not working. I imagine if I had their job, I would too. "What's going on?" I ask.

"For fuck's sake!" Caroline says, standing up and rushing over to me. She pulls me into a hug and squeezes me tight. "We've been worried sick about you, Maddie."

Diane is up now too, her sunglasses low down on the bridge of her nose as she looks at me through thick, fake eyelashes. Which suddenly makes me think of Raquel and the other girls at Pete's. Which makes me remember that Pete's is gone. That *Pete* is gone. And I'll probably never see those girls again.

God. How things have changed. I feel equal parts sad and happy about the change. Because on the one hand, I feel like I'm out of the rut I was in. And on the other... I feel like I gave up a lot to get here.

Caroline holds me out at arm's length, looking me over like I need a good looking-over. "You're OK? You were in Monaco?"

Monaco? "Uh, yeah, I'm fine. How'd you know I was in... Monaco?"

Diane huffs some air, which blows her hair up around her eyes, and then points to the table under the palapa and says, "Sit down and have a drink with us."

I relent. Not because I want to have a drink with them—I really just want to grab some clothes and go back to Evan and Robert's place and get back into bed with Tyler. I know if I'm gone too long he'll get antsy and that's not a good thing. He might decide he's recovered and start doing something stupid like... I dunno. Take your pick of things Tyler could be doing that he shouldn't be doing. It's highly unlikely he's in bed right now.

"Just one," I say to Diane. But she's already walking into the house to blend up something cool and fruity for me.

"How's Tyler?" Caroline asks. "Diane said he was pretty upset when she saw him. Are you guys OK? Is everything...?"

I open my mouth to answer, then stop, because my answer was going to be about the state of his bruised—not broken—ribs. But I catch myself just in time. "Oh, yeah, he's fine. We're fine," I say instead.

"You don't seem convinced," Diane says, returning, plopping down next to Caroline and sliding a strawberry daiquiri towards me. She eyes me. "What's really going on? We haven't seen you in I don't know how long." She sips her own drink.

"It's not that we're prying," Caroline says. "It's that, well... We're lonely."

Diane huffs out another breath of air, once again blowing her bangs away from her eyes. Her sunglasses are on top of her head now, so I can see her better.

I realize she might've been crying.

"Are you guys OK?" I ask, suddenly feeling awful for not asking about them first.

"Perfect," Diane quips back. "I mean we're just great. We lost one of our best friends, and now we're about to lose another one. What could be better than that?"

Best friend? Another one? Does she mean me?

I just stare at them for a few seconds, trying to wrap my head around this new development. They are friends, I decide. They took me in when I had nowhere to go. They accepted me and made me feel welcome. And yeah, some of that was just practicality. They had an empty room, I had rent money. But we're more than that. Aren't we?

"I know you're a loner," Diane says, wiping her eyes. She's crying for sure now, but not like sobs or anything. Just tears. "I get it. You're a survivor. And you don't need anyone. You built your life around self-reliance. But we're pack people, ya know? Caroline and me. And now Annie's gone and you're... you're gonna leave us too, aren't you?"

"No," I say automatically. But I regret it immediately. Because yes. I am.

"Are you done stripping?" Caroline asks.

I nod, inhale deeply, then let the breath out slowly. "Yeah, I'm done. I don't know what I'm gonna do next but... Pete's, ya know? It was... I can't explain it, I guess. But it was necessary and now..."

"And now you're moving on," Diane finishes. Her tears have been wiped away, her stoic exterior back in place.

I nod. "Yeah, I guess I am."

"We're happy for you," Caroline says. "And for Annie too. I mean, who the hell wants their best friends to be stuck wasting their only lives as whores, right?"

"Caroline," I start. But I have nothing for that. She's right. No one chooses to sell their body if they don't have to. I need to say something kind to my friends. Because that's what they are. Maybe we're not your classic girl gang, but we're in this together.

At least we were. Before Annie left town to find her happily ever after. Before I found my long-lost soulmate and he ended up being a bazillionaire. Which makes my current situation kind of fairytale too, doesn't it?

If I wasn't sitting next to two thoroughly distressed women, I'd laugh out loud at that. Because after all the pain, and the fear, and the anger, and the failure—I found something good. And it had nothing to do with anything but luck.

Diane and Caroline didn't get the good luck. They're still here, in exactly the same place they were. Stuck. Two college-educated women selling sex to make ends meet.

It's not fair.

But when has life ever been fair?

There's several moments of awkward silence. "So," I say, trying to fill the empty space. "What do you guys have planned for the future?"

"If you move out, then I guess our future involves looking for a second new roommate." Diane says this without hiding her animosity.

Old Maddie would be irritated with her for projecting her failures into my happiness, but I'm not Old Maddie. So I sympathize. "Look, you guys, you're not stuck, OK? Stuck is a state of mind."

"That's easy for you to say," Diane says, taking a long sip of her drink.

I take a sip of mine, then almost choke from the rum. "That's strong," I say, eyes watering and throat burning.

"Not strong enough if you ask me," Diane mutters back.

"Stuck isn't a state of mind," Caroline says. "It's just reality, Maddie. And don't mind Diane, she's just upset because we feel like... like every time things start going good something happens to derail us, ya know?"

Boy, can I ever relate.

"And it's not like we're unhappy for you and Annie. You two deserve happiness."

"We all deserve happiness," I say.

"Yeah," Diane says. "But we don't all get lucky and find it, do we?"

"Look," I say, and now it's my turn to blow out a huff of breath. "You both have degrees, for Christ's sake. What did you major in?"

"Economics," Caroline says. "Both of us. But the market fell and job opportunities weren't good and—"

"And now things are better!" I say brightly.

27

"Sure," Diane says. "But we've spent the last few years as fucking prostitutes trying to pay off student loans. Uh, no one is going to be hiring us as financial advisors now."

She's right. Once you make a mistake like prostitution, it stays with you. Maybe not forever, but every bad decision digs you a little bit deeper into the hole. You gotta claw your way back up with a vengeance to have any hope of getting a second chance. It's not what human resources is looking for when picking job candidates.

"Why did you guys go with that anyway?" I ask, probably not cautiously enough.

Diane glares at me. "Asks the stripper." Yeah. That's pretty fucking fair.

"There's always a way." I sigh. "You just need to be creative."

"Like you?" Diane says, getting up and walking away. Then she calls over her shoulder, "Good luck, Maddie. I really mean that," as she goes inside.

"Sorry," Caroline says. "She's just… down these days. She'll come out of it. She always does."

Yeah. What choice does she have, right? Give up or keep fighting. That's all there is to life. And Diane is right. I was creative. I mean, I had a new idea practically every week. But none of them paid off. Not even the drone, even though it was a good idea in the end. I've failed at every creative venture I tried. Tyler's the one who found fortune, not me. I'm just a tagalong.

"Well," I say, getting up. "I gotta grab some clothes and stuff and get back to Tyler before he does something dumb."

Caroline laughs as she gets up too. She hugs me tight and says, "Don't be a stranger, OK? I'm gonna miss you more than you think."

I smile at her. Sweet, sweet Caroline. I wish I could make everything perfect for her. But I can't. So I don't even try. "I promise," I say. "I won't."

Back in my bedroom—which is actually neat since Tyler picked it up one day weeks ago and I haven't had time to mess it all up again—I pack. At first I only pack a few outfits to get me through the week, but the thought of coming back here every few days just to get more clothes changes my mind.

I don't want to be a stranger, but I don't want to be here either.

So I pack up all my clothes that don't have Scarlett written on them. I take down the few photos I had tacked to a bulletin board. Scotty and me. Us and the parents when we were kids. One of me and Annie from college, which I stole from her, because I have no pictures of myself during that time. And a few of all four of us—me, Caroline, Diane, and Annie—taking selfies during rare moments of happiness right after I moved in.

An hour later my room looks... cold. Impersonal. Ready for the next tenant who comes through here.

I'm not moving out.

I tell myself this over and over again.

But I *am* moving on.

TYLER

Five stars.

That's what I give the dude who drops me off at Mandalay. Five stars. Because that's what you do. You give everybody a five-star rating. Unless the driver gets into an accident or, like, verbally assaults you or whatever. Otherwise, tap! Five stars!

So stupid. That's what the world has become. Just assholes giving their online opinions of other assholes. Because when you rate a driver, or a dry cleaner, or a restaurant or whatever, it's not like a thoughtful or nuanced critique. It's just an opinion. I liked it or I didn't like it. It was good or it was bad. Not a study of your experience, not an assessing of the dimensions of your experience, not a consideration of your own role in the dynamics of a thing. Just a *feeling*. Fuckin' hell. Everybody and their fucking feelings. Jesus.

But at least I can do everything on my phone now and don't have to carry money and shit. It's like the whole world has become a hotel room. Because doing all this shit on our phones is like ordering room service. No money changes hands and you don't even think about it, but then at the end of the month when the credit card bill comes, you're like, *I spent five thousand dollars on moo goo gai pan? What the fuck?*

Whatever.

I'm only kicking all this shit around right now to avoid going inside. I'm not even sure what I'm doing here. No. Yeah, I am. This is one of those things I have to do if I'm gonna be fresh-start, new-look Tyler. I have to deal with my dad. I goddamn have to. That he came to Evan, looking for me, just forces my hand. Because I'm real, real curious about what would compel him to show up out of the blue. I don't know the guy at all anymore, but the guy I knew wouldn't do something like that. Not for me, anyway. I mean, he didn't come looking for me for twelve years.

I don't even really know how that happened. It just kinda did. I tried staying in touch when I went off to basic. I'd call him and, like, send emails and shit, but he was always too busy to talk, and he'd NEVER take the time to return an email, and eventually I just decided fuck it. I engaged with it like an experiment. *Let's see – if I don't reach out to him – how long it will take him to think to try to reach out to find me.*

Forever, it turns out, would be the answer.

And all of a sudden, I feel a little sick. Because I never saw it before right this very moment.

I'm just like my fucking dad. Fuck me.

I ghosted in the same goddamn way. I know I'm different than him in that I at least concocted a bunch of bullshit rationales to justify why I disappeared on the world, but I'm not sure if that makes me better or worse. One thing I can give my dad credit for, if I'm being generous (and fuck it, it's the holidays), is that he's never pretended to be anything other than the unconscionable cocksucker he is.

But shit. He wasn't always. I mean, it was so long ago that it almost feels like it was somebody else's life, but I have this weird, vague memory of things that I didn't totally hate about him. Like, I remember the first time I ever had pizza, it was just me and him. I don't know where Mom was. But I must've been about six and he picked me up from school because there was a burst water main or something, and we went and got pizza. And maybe it's just the foggy haze of memory, but I don't think I've had a slice that tasted that good since.

I also remember him coming into my room, when I was maybe even smaller, after I had had a bad dream or something, and crawling into my bunk (I slept in the top bunk of my bunk bed even though there was nobody sleeping in the bunk below. I just liked being up above everything), calming me down and reading a Batman comic to me.

But then, I also remember when Mom got sick, how he changed. How he couldn't handle it. How he started drinking and fucking disappearing on us for, like, the whole weekend. And how for almost three years, it felt like it was just me and Mom. I was the one toweling her mouth off after she'd throw up from the treatments. And I was the one sitting with her in the hospital when she had tubes and shit dripping poison into her. Because when you're talking about treating cancer, you're just trading one poison for another in the hopes that the man-made one can overpower the natural one. Man versus nature. The lesser of two evils.

Mom used to try to tell me that he was just dealing in his own way. Always seemed to me that he wasn't dealing at all. And then she died. And whatever remnants of "good guy" he had in him died along with her.

Those five or so years when it was just me and him made me who I am, I now realize. I learned a lot about myself during that time. Mostly I learned that drunk people are hard to reason with and that you'll have to be ready to fucking kill me if you want to trade fists, because I won't back down, I won't quit, and I will keep coming until you won't be able to tell whose blood is whose.

Guy got me ready for battle, I'll give him that much.

Which brings me back to why I'm here today. If I'm here to put the past behind me and get closure with him, or forgive him, or myself, or whatever I hope to accomplish, I figured I should do it here, at his work, instead of at home where all those memories might just cause me to forget that they're in the past too. The mind is a funny thing. It makes you believe that some shit that used to be true is still true now.

That's what makes fighting so satisfying. When you're being attacked with a knife, you aren't worrying about being attacked with a knife. You're just fucking reacting and scrambling to stay alive. It keeps you from dwelling on the past, on worrying about the future. You're too busy focusing on survival. It's a great way to distract yourself.

But it's time to let that shit go. It really is. I'm all fought out, I think. And Maddie deserves better. So it's time to be better. Better than my dad, at least. Which is a low friggin' bar, but on the plus side, it means it should be easy to hurdle.

OK. Let's fuckin' do this.

Walking inside a casino always takes me a minute or two. Especially in the middle of the day. It's tough for me to get my bearings because there's so much going on.

Sounds, and sights, and smoke and perfume and desperation. It's a lot.

I flag down a cocktail waitress. "'Scuse me, is Jack Morgan around?"

"Jack? Sure, yeah, I think so. Hold on." And she goes off to find him.

I assume everybody knows him. He's been here since the place opened. Only reason I know this is where he still works is because he scurried away back over here after we saw him in the lobby of the Four Seasons. So funny—if I had even stopped to think that he might have been here, I probably would've put Maddie's parents up at a different hotel. And then I wouldn't have run off back to Evan's, and Maddie wouldn't have come after me to make sure I was all right, and she might not have had the interaction with Robert that led us to the Hoover Dam, which is the night it really feels like we locked into this thing we're into now, and the night that Pete's burned down, which bonded us even more tightly, and brought us to this place where we are now. This place where I want to be with her all the time and always. And to do that, I need to start living my life in a quieter, more peaceful, more forgiving way. And to do that, I have to confront my father.

A butterfly flaps its wings and halfway around the world Tyler Morgan talks with his dad for the first time in twelve years.

"Here he is." The waitress's voice comes from behind me. Because of course it does. Because there's no way this could just be semi-normal, where he walks across the floor, sees me, and we both have a moment to prepare for the fact that I'm here. Of course it has to be this big fucking dramatic reveal where I turn around and he sees me, and the expression on his face changes and it's like a scene out of a goddamn Hallmark Hall of Fame movie or some shit. Because this is my life.

So, I turn around, and yep, all that shit happens.

Classic.

Finally, finally, after me staring at him for half a minute as the world continues to whizz by around us, he says, "Hey. Uh..." And that's it.

Solid start, Pops.

"You went to see Evan about me?" I figure I'll just get this show on the road.

"Uh, yeah. I did."

I wait. I nod. Finally, "And? What do you need?"

"Nothin'. Nothin'. It was just Christmas and I... Nothin'."

Three nothin's in one sentence equals somethin'. That's just math.

Finally, I take a breath and decide to try this "being the bigger man" shit. And not just physically. "How you been, Jack?"

He takes a half-step toward me. It's an uncertain, shaky half-step, but he's that much closer. Not sure how that makes me feel. "Um, I dunno. OK. I been OK. You?"

I nod a little. Purse my lips. "I'm alive. So it feels like I'm ahead of the game."

I remember Jeff's funeral and how I wondered, if I had died, would Jack Morgan even have known? Would he have cared? And then I push that memory away, because it ain't helping right now.

"Tyler, I—"

"What do you do here now? You still a pit boss?" That used to drive him crazy. It's actually called "pit manager," but I knew it made him cringe when I called him a "boss," so I said it all the fucking time. (I don't do it now to piss him off. It's just habit.)

"No," he says, more gently than I would've imagined him reacting. "No, I'm, uh, I'm a shift manager now. I oversee the whole operation while I'm here."

I raise my eyebrows and nod again. "Good for you."

"Tyler... You wanna maybe go to my office, or—?"

"No, I'm good."

Silence. Well, between us anyway. The sound of the casino continues to play its gambler's melody in the background.

"I think about you all the time," he says.

"Yeah? You do? What do you think?"

"I think..." He rubs his hand over his mouth. "I think... I fucked up. Real, real bad. I think that I gave you a terrible childhood, on top of the fact that your mom died. I just made things that much worse."

I purse my lips again and shrug. "OK. Well, we're on the same page about that."

He sighs. "And that by the time I pulled myself together to, I dunno, reach out, you were gone. And I figured the last thing you'd want is to see me again, so..."

"So you decided not to try."

He nods sheepishly. Another long beat passes.

"It's fucked up that you didn't even recognize me." I don't know why I say it. It's just what comes out.

He wags his head back and forth. "I know. I mean, it was out of the fuckin' blue, and that beard is... Fuck. No. No excuse. It was fucked up. I'm sorry."

Three things occur to me now:

One, I don't think I've ever heard Jack Morgan apologize for anything.

Two, this feels a lot like I'm on the other side of the exact same scenario that happened with me and Maddie. Except for all the sex, obviously.

And three, I realize what this really is. I'm now the dad. And he's the kid who screwed up and is standing in front of me wondering what kind of punishment I'm going to give him.

The whole thing just makes me sad. I'm not feeling vindicated or purified or whatever I was hoping to feel. I just feel... yeah. Sad.

"You seeing anybody?" I ask him.

He shakes his head. "Nah. No. Not right now."

"You ever get married again?"

"No. No. I mean, I don't wanna get all... But your mom was the only woman I could ever see myself being married to like that. She filled in all the fucked-up places in me that needed to be filled. I don't think I'll ever find that again." He's looking at the floor as he says it, then he lifts his eyes to me. "I mean it."

My breathing speeds up and gets a little shallow. I don't know why. Or I do, but I don't wanna get into it.

"You?" he asks. "You married?"

I actually laugh at that. "Me? Ha. Yeah, fuck no."

"Yeah," he says on a tiny laugh. Like maybe this is a place where we understand each other. Like who the fuck would have us, right? Then he says, "You kept up with the Claytons?"

Shit. I didn't even think that he would ask about that. But of course he would. We're making fucking small talk and the only thing he knows about my life at all is that he saw me on Thanksgiving with the Clayton posse.

"Nah, not really. Maddie and I just ran into each other a couple months back and... Nah. Not really." Yeah. That seems like just about all I want to share on the subject.

He nods. Then he says, "I dunno what to do, Ty. I don't even know where to start."

Yeah. No shit. "Um, well, like, here," I offer. "This is what some might call a start." Again, I'm not really planning what I'm going to say, shit's just coming out of my mouth.

"Yeah?" he says. "Is it? You wanna...? I dunno. Something?"

I cross my arms in front of my chest completely involuntarily. "I dunno, Jack. What would 'something' look like?"

"Yeah. I dunno either, but... You doing anything for New Year's?"

I eyeball him carefully. "Why?"

"You like Maroon 5?"

Maroon fucking 5? "Not really. Why?"

"Oh, they're just playing here, and I thought I could get you tickets and... Whatever. No big deal." And he looks at the floor again. Shit. Watching him, I see all the similarities between him and me, and it makes me... I dunno if there's a word. "Was there something you wanted?" he asks. "From me? Particularly?"

I think about that. And while I'm thinking, some drunk-in-the-day tourist bumps into my side and I grab at it and grimace.

"You OK?" asks Jack, stepping over to me. "You hurt or something?"

"No, no, man, I'm good," I say, backing up and waving him off. It's wild. The way he stepped to me resembled some fatherly, protector impulse or something.

It's kinda freaking me out. He puts up his hands and backs off.

"No," I say, in response to his question about wanting something from him. "No, dude, I don't want anything. I'm thinking about maybe changing some shit up in my life, y'know? Like looking at what the rest of my life is gonna look like, and... I dunno. I guess I was just trying to see if a path forward might have you in it." Again, shit is just coming out of my mouth that I had absolutely no intention of saying.

"I'd like that," he says. "I mean..." He starts to say something else but chokes it off. He does this like three times before he finally just says, "Yeah. I'd like that."

I nod a bit, making kind of clicking sounds with my tongue. "So what the fuck do we...?"

"Well, I mean, there's an awful, awful lot to catch up on. You maybe wanna come over for dinner, and...?"

"You still living in the house?" I ask. He nods. "Yeah, then maybe not just yet. Not sure I wanna, y'know, see whatever you did with my old room and shit."

"Oh, I—" But I put up another hand to stop him.

"Don't wanna know. Doesn't matter."

"Fair enough." He sucks in a breath. "I could come over to your place. Where you living?"

"Why don't we just meet up somewhere?"

"Oh. OK. Frank's?"

Frank's is where we used to go grab milkshakes. Mom loved it. It's just an old-school diner with vinyl seats and the open pass-through into the kitchen and all that shit. I don't even think I realized it was still around. But, hell, if we're going for nostalgia, may as well go all in.

"Sure. Yeah. We can do that."

"Next week sometime?" he asks.

"Can we do it before the new year? I'm trying to... Can we just do it before the new year?" I don't feel like explaining that I'm trying to start the new year fresh, because it's nobody's fucking business what I'm doing. If he and I are gonna... whatever... I just wanna put our past behind us now.

"Yeah, sure," he says. "Um, I'm tied up tomorrow and the next day. Day after?"

"The thirtieth? Sure. Done. Time?"

"I dunno. Like... four o'clock?"

"Frank's, four o'clock on the thirtieth. Super."

I don't wait around for the awkward goodbye, and God knows I'm not looking for a hug or a goddamn handshake or anything like that, so I just walk past him and head for the exit. But something... I dunno what, just something... is gnawing at me. So I turn back. "Hey!" He turns to look in the direction of my shout. "When you came looking for me. With Evan... It was just because it was Christmas?"

There's a long, long pause. Too long, if I stop to consider it. And then, finally, he nods at me and says, "Yeah."

I wrap my hand into a fist around my beard and stroke it a couple of times. "K."

Then I nod briskly and head outside, pulling out my phone as I go so that I can request a car and catch myself another goddamn five-star ride.

CHAPTER FOUR

MADDIE

On the way home from my old house, I swing by Plumeria's office. I don't know why I do it. I just... I just need someone to talk to, I guess. And even though I know she's probably got clients and has no time for me, I figure it's almost lunch time and, well, what can it hurt, right?

Her door is closed when I get there. She shares her office with other therapists, who all share a receptionist, and even though I don't really want to wait, the receptionist is so certain Plumeria will want to see me after her current appointment, I relent and take a seat in the waiting room and thumb through an old copy of *Cosmo*.

Fifteen minutes later her door opens and she leads a patient out. She sees me but says nothing until her patient has left.

"Maddie," she says, walking towards me once she's free. "This is an unexpected surprise."

"Sorry," I say, standing up and fidgeting with the hem of my t-shirt. "I was in the neighborhood and—" But I sigh, then shrug, then tell her the truth. "Do you have time? I'd really like to have a chat."

"Uh... sure. Have a seat in my office while I grab my lunch and we can catch up while I eat."

I do as she says and a few minutes later she joins me, not sitting at her desk, but next to me on the long comfortable couch.

"So what's up?" she asks. "Everything OK?"

"Well," I say. "Yes and no. I'm really not sure." Even though there's a lot I could tell her about Carlos, and Logan, and the whole undercover DEA thing down in Mexico, none of that is what's troubling me now. So I don't even bother. Instead I say, "You know how I was stuck?"

Plumeria is chewing her sandwich, nodding her head at me.

"Well... I feel like I'm unstuck."

"That's great," she says, swallowing her food. "I'm so happy to hear that. What's changed?"

"Tyler?" I say, unsure. "The guy I was holding responsible for Scotty, even though he had nothing to do with it. Mostly him."

"So you've got a new guy?"

"Yeah, he's someone both Scotty and I knew. You remember him, right? Tyler Morgan?"

"Yeah," she says. "Sure. Went off to the military?"

"That's him. Well, he and I are seeing each other now."

"That's great. Right?" She looks at me.

"It is," I agree. "But..." I sigh, then take a deep breath. "But things are going well."

"And?" she asks, after several seconds of silence from me.

"And I was living with these other girls, you know, while I was struggling."

"OK."

"And one of them is also doing well. She moved back to Kansas or Iowa or wherever she's from. You know, to give her old life a second chance. But the other two friends, well, they're kinda stuck, ya know?"

"So you feel guilty? Because you and this friend found something good and they haven't?"

"Exactly," I say. "Yes. I feel like maybe I don't deserve all this sudden good fortune and I'm not better than they are, and yet... here I am. Tyler Morgan is a millionaire now."

"Is he?" Plu says.

I nod. "Yeah. Like fuckin' loaded."

"Hmmm," she says.

"What's that mean?" I ask. "Hmmm?"

"Well," she says. "You feel lucky."

"Yes!" I say. "And luck, ya know... it's just..."

"Luck," she finishes for me.

"Exactly."

"And that feels unfair. That you've found something good and your friends, who deserve luck just as much as you, haven't."

"Yes."

"That's called guilt. You need to appreciate that love happens to people who look for it. Who accept it. You went looking for things. Never content to stay still, never satisfied with your sadness. And even if you didn't know it, you were making your own luck when you did this. Your friends need to do that too. The one who left town, to go give her old life a second chance. Where would she be if she never took that risk?"

"Here," I say. "Stuck with them."

"So she made her luck as well."

"But nothing about me has changed, Plu. I'm still the same mess I was a few months ago. Now I just have a partner in crime, so to speak. Someone to be lost *with*."

She smiles at me, like that was the exact right thing to say.

"It's just luck," I insist. "Tyler came home, we found each other by accident, and then… and then…"

"And then you both gave it a chance."

"Is that all there is to it?"

"Sometimes good things happen, Maddie. For no fathomable reason. Just like the bad things. You just accept it and move on. That's all you can do."

"But what about my friends?"

"You want to help them?"

"If I can," I say.

"Can you?" she asks.

Which makes me sigh. "I dunno."

"Well, not everyone wants to be helped." She tilts her head at me, the way she does, and continues. "I recall a certain someone who came into my office not so long ago who refused all help. From every direction."

I nod, smiling a little.

"So whatever it was that made you change your mind… that's what those friends need to find as well."

"But I don't know what that was."

"Don't you?"

"I mean, sure. It was Tyler. But—"

She shakes her head at me. "It wasn't Tyler, Maddie. It was *you*."

I think about that the whole drive back to Evan and Robert's house, but it makes no sense. Love changed me.

I can't find love for people. I mean, sure, I did decide to give Tyler a chance, but that was because he and I truly are meant to be together.

So it still makes no sense.

But I have this feeling of dread hanging over me now. A feeling of foreboding. I'm sure that I can write some of it off to the fact that my life has been totally flipped upside down in the last couple of months, and I can write some of it off to the fact that I'm still really un-used to feeling safe. And happy.

But I think mostly it's the feeling that I'm starting to get all the things I feel like I've wanted in my life — love, companionship, someone who really gets me — and I'm worried that the rug is just gonna get pulled out from under me again. Because that's what happens to people, right? They get comfortable, and then they get complacent, and then, bam, the universe sucker-punches them.

I don't know. I feel like I'm thinking too much. Maybe being around Tyler is rubbing off on me in ways I didn't expect. Or maybe it's just that, like I told Plu, I still feel guilty.

How do I help my friends? How do I make them keep climbing? Keep hoping? Keep looking for whatever it is that's missing in their lives?

I dunno. But they helped me. They might not know it, but they did.

So I'm gonna figure it out. I owe them that much, at least.

No, I feel good. I do. I know I do.

I just don't know why my knuckles are white as I grip the steering wheel.

CHAPTER FIVE

MADDIE & TYLER

MADDIE

"Thanks," I tell the delivery girl as I take the food from her. Tyler's over by the open accordion doors that turn Evan and Robert's place into an indoor/outdoor space, trying to fan the smoke out of the house. I walked away for five minutes while we were making dinner so that I could take a call from Mom and Dad, and when I walked back into the kitchen, the whole range top was on fire.

I don't know how he does it.

So we ordered some Chinese food, using an app on Tyler's phone. The delivery girl is extra-sweet, so I give her five stars and a big tip. Then as I'm closing the app, I glance and see why she was extra-sweet. "Dude, do you have any idea how much money you've spent on delivery from this place in the last year?"

"No. Why?" he says, waving what looks like a very expensive, crystal serving tray around to fan the smoke.

"Because," I say, jogging to him and taking from him the priceless glass smoke-blower he's about to break, and handing him a brown paper bag filled with a container of sesame noodles. "It's more than most people pay in rent."

"Really?" he asks, looking at the floor.

I put the tray down on the dining room table, then take the bag and put it down as well. Stroking his arm, I say, "Hey. Hey, I'm just fucking with you. What's wrong?"

He doesn't say anything for a moment, just bobs his head. Then, "Saw my dad today."

That's an attention-grabber. "What? You did? Where?" I pull him to the outside part of the indoor/outdoor space and sit him in a lounge chair. I sit across from him, but I don't let go of his hands.

"At his work. Went to see him."

"Wha—? Why? I didn't know you were going to do that."

"I didn't either. I mean, I did. I just didn't necessarily plan on doing it today. I was going to talk with you about it. Like, get your thoughts and figure out exactly what I was going to say, but then Evan told me that he came looking for me while you and I were...on vacation..." He moves his shoulders around like he knows this should be funny but can't bring himself to laugh, so I laugh for him. It makes him smile. "And I just, I dunno. Decided to go see him."

"Why didn't you tell me before?"

He shrugs. "Dunno. Figured we'd make dinner, sit, eat, talk about our days like normal-ass people." Then he mumbles something that sounds like 'new-look Tyler,' and sighs out a huge breath.

"Hey," I say, bending my head down to make him look me in the eyes. "Hey, look at me." He does. "We will never. Ever. In a million years. Be normal-ass people. Not as long as you're involved in the conversation. And I'm so fucking glad about that." I smile, and it makes him smile again. "OK?" He nods. Then, "So now what?"

"I dunno." He cuts me off. "He and I are sitting down in a couple of days though."

In the little bit of time we've been back in each other's lives (although it seems MUCH longer), I have seen Tyler in a lot of different states. I've seen him sad, angry, despondent, intense, romantic, sexy, and (my favorite, especially when we're naked together) happy. Right now, he is something I've not even glimpsed before: scared.

It's not a shuddering, simmering kind of fear. It's tinged with nervousness. Anxiety. But it's a brand of fear, nonetheless. I hold his hands tighter.

"Do you... want me to go with you?" I ask.

He shakes his head, but says, "Maybe."

"OK. OK. You'll let me know, yeah?"

He nods.

It's quiet now. He's lost in his thoughts, and I don't feel like I want to pry too much more. The one thing I know about Tyler Morgan is that when he wants to talk he will talk and when he doesn't, he won't. So I do what a good partner does. I change the subject.

"How are your ribs there, killer?"

He looks at me with surprise.

"Oh, come on. You're worse at hiding things than I am. And I'm terrible." More smiling. We're both giving a stab at happiness all we've got.

"I'm fine," he mumbles out.

"Yeah? Well, you know what I think we should do?" I ask, getting up out of my chair to kneel between his legs and putting my hand on his crotch.

"I think I have some idea," he says, an evil smirk dancing on his lips.

51

JA HUSS & JOHNATHAN McCLAIN

"I think we should get in the hot tub and give that aching body some love."

He looks half disappointed and says, "But we'll still fuck, right?"

"Yes, Tyler. We will still fuck." I sigh. I fuckin' love this guy.

Completely.

TYLER

She stretches up and kisses me. Or I lean down and kiss her. Whatever. We kiss. I fuckin' love this girl. Completely.

She takes me by the hand and leads me over to the hot tub, which is lit up and steaming, mist floating up into the night sky. She unzips her jeans and shimmies them down her legs, pulls her t-shirt up over her head and stands there in a dark green bra and thong.

"Holy shit," I say. "Christmas never ends." She closes her eyes and grins. I continue, by doing what everyone knows is the worst thing you can do to a joke. Explaining. "I'm saying, because your hair is red and your underwear—"

"Yeah, I got it, babe."

She nods towards me, which is my cue to disrobe as well. I also unzip my jeans and let them fall to the ground. I'm now standing there in just a t-shirt, my cock already at full mast.

"Let me help you. Don't want you to stretch too much." She glides over. I wonder if she knows that her regular walk looks like she's gliding down a runway at all times. Runways of Paris, runway of Pete's. Doesn't matter.

She has this beautiful, effortless stride that makes her impossible not to notice.

She grabs the hem of my t-shirt and pulls me toward her. One hand on my dick, one hand on my chest, she draws me in for another kiss.

"Babe," she says, her voice a whisper, her lips barely touching mine.

"Hmm?" I hum back.

"When are you gonna shave?"

I wouldn't call that a buzzkill, but it's definitely a buzz-assault.

"Why? You're really done with it?"

"I dunno," she says, all coy and shit, her fingers on my lips. "You're just talking about making a fresh start and... You know. It'd be nice. To feel skin"—she takes my hand and plunges it down the front of her panties, so that I can feel her dampening flesh—"on skin," she whispers in my ear.

"Yeah, OK, you got it, I'll shave. Should we see if Rodney's in now?"

She laughs. At my sudden agreeability, I guess. But she also tips her chin back and asks, "Who's Rodney?"

"You remember Mustache? From Thanksgiving? The salon guy?"

"Oh, yeah. The one who clearly wanted some of this." She squeezes my cock harder and I moan.

"Mmmm, yup. That's him."

She starts stroking me back and forth with one hand and forcing my hand to stroke her clit with the other. "Yeah, I think maybe we'll just call Rodney in the morning. Let's give the beard a proper send-off tonight."

I pull us close together with my free hand and execute the patented Tyler Morgan one-hand bra release. She gasps, then giggles, then steps back, bending me forward and pulling my t-shirt off so that I don't have to lift my arms over my head.

Once the shirt is off, she stays back a step and works her panties down her legs. We stand, naked, facing each other, as the steam from the hot tub floats in the air around us.

"You're beautiful," I tell her.

"Ditto, mister," she says. "C'mere." We join hands and descend into the warm, bubbling water. I sit and go to bring her down into my lap, but she stops me, says, "Unh-unh-unh, Adam," and turns to face me.

Screwing up my face, I ask, "Fuck's Adam? Did you just call me Adam? Do I have to kill somebody else?" (That's a risky punchline, but I think she'll appreciate it.)

She rolls her eyes. "Like Adam and Eve? With the rib? And, like, your ribs are...? And I'm naked and you're naked and this is amazing and shit, like Eden?" She gestures around us. I'm tempted to tell her not to explain a joke, but in this case it actually helped.

"Oh, yes, right. My ribs. Got it. Ha, ha. You're a regular Elayne Boosler."

She splashes water in my face. "Just shut up, sit on the edge, and behave." I do. I prop myself on the edge of the tub so that just my calves are in the water. The chilly desert air against the warm beads of moisture on my now wet body feels amazing.

But not as amazing as her lips on my cock as she plops her knees on the seat inside the hot tub and goes down on me.

MADDIE

The warm water undulating around my body, splashing my tits, as I work his dick with my lips feels like I'm on a drug. And when he reaches out and pinches my nipples, it feels like an overdose. As I pump the base of his shaft with my hand, my head bobs and twists and licks his thick cock as, under the water, I finger myself desperately.

I keep pumping on him with my hand and let my mouth now find his balls. They're swollen and full, and I put both of them in my mouth at once (which is no small task) and build the pressure, allowing the suction of my tongue to tug his sack away from his body. Like I'm trying to devour him.

The splashing of the water from the hand that I'm fingering myself with becomes more violent and the jerking and sucking intensifies in kind. "Oh, God. Oh, my fuck," he lets out as his hands tangle themselves in my hair and he yanks my head back, my mouth wrenching from his body with a gasp.

Panting, I say, "What?"

He says nothing, just pushes me back, stands up, turns me around, and thrusts himself inside me. "Oh, shit!" It's the only appropriate thing to exclaim.

We're both standing in the water to our thighs and each thrust he makes sounds like the lapping of waves on a shore. It reminds me of the other night (was it only just the other night?) when we were hidden by the dune in Ensenada. So desperate and in need of one another, so reckless but at the same time as careful as we could be not to get caught.

There is no such prohibition here.

In this beautiful home, on this crystal-clear night, with no neighbors for a thousand yards in any direction, we can be as reckless as we want. Urgent. Needy. Primal. For the first time since we had sex in his apartment on Halloween, we are actually alone.

We're not in an alley where someone can find us, or my place where my roommates might walk in, or a hotel room with my parents in the lobby, or even hidden under the Hoover Dam with Terry the security guard promising not to watch us on security cameras but knowing damn well that he probably is. For only the second time ever, it's just us.

The only other time we were completely alone, I cried during sex for the first time in my life. I know it was because it was wrapped up with a lot of other things. Halloween, and feeling trapped, and wanting so much for this thing with this "Ford" guy to work. (Ha. Ford.) And then it all went bad. And then it somehow got better. And then it got terrible. And now here we are. In this Eden, all alone, like we really are the only two people on earth. And while that's not true, it's a nice way to think of now.

"Fuck me, fuck me, fuck me harder," I command. And he obliges.

He's grunting and panting and pulling me towards him. I have my hands on the edge of the hot tub so that I can assist him by pushing back every time he pulls. It's so unyielding and savage that you'd think we hadn't had sex in ten years. As opposed to twice this morning.

The water is splashing all around us now, spraying up into the sky, the droplets mingling with the steam and mist. It's beautiful. It is the very spirit of our bewildering and impenetrable love for each other lifting towards the sky. It is passion rising, and it is carrying us with it.

"Oh, fuck, babe, I'm gonna come," he pants.

"Me too, baby. I am too. Come with me? Please? I want you to come with me."

His breathing is fast and shallow and so is mine as he pitches into me. And when we both come, the wailing moan from him and the frenzied scream from me blend into one sound. The sound of us echoing out of Eden and into the vastness of forever.

TYLER

"The food's probably cold," I say into the top of her head. We're sitting in the water. She's leaning against me, her head on my chest, and it really doesn't hurt. Either this hot tub is mad therapeutic, or her pussy has healing powers. Possibly a little of both.

"I'm good," she purrs, stroking her fingers on my chest, tracing my scars.

"Yeah." I sigh.

She sits up and looks at me. "What? Are you thinking about your dad again?"

"No. Not exactly. Kind of? I dunno."

"What's going on?" She sits up even further.

"Just... Honestly? Thinking about how much I spend on ordering food makes me feel really shitty."

"Why?"

"Because when we were in Mexico all I could think about was how fucking privileged and entitled Carlos is. Was. Whatever. Just, of all the ways I think the guy was a piece of shit, one of them is that he had all this fucking money that he made off of someone else's suffering."

"OK," she says, "but that's not—"

"Isn't it?" I interrupt. "Because privilege and entitlement is privilege and entitlement whether you're using your money to run drugs and hold women against their will, or you're just sitting around ordering an ass-load of crispy noodles with duck sauce." She eyes me dubiously. "OK. So maybe it's not *exactly* the same, but it still makes me feel like crap. It's all tied up with seeing my dad. Fuck. He's selfish and shitty just like me. But then, today, he seemed like he was genuinely remorseful. Like he really wants to try to set things right. To put the past behind him, just like I do. And even though something in the pit of my stomach is telling me to be careful, I really want to believe."

"Well. That's good. Right?"

"I dunno. Just... to be reminded that all I've done for the last however long is a whole lotta nothing just makes me mad at myself. Because I don't deserve what I've got right now. I know I don't. You, your forgiveness, your love, your generosity of spirit. All this." I gesture around us. "My life."

"Hey! Stop that." She tugs on my beard. I think she'll miss it more than she realizes.

"No," I say. "Seriously. What's fucked up is that I thought for a really long time that I deserved to find happiness. Or something. That I'd earned it."

"You have."

"Bullshit. I don't deserve half of what I've got." Those steps we climb to get where we're going? More often than not, they're built on top of the discarded bodies of the less fortunate. I remember thinking that and feeling like, *Oh, well, that's life*, and just accepting it as the truth. And maybe it is. But it doesn't have to be.

She takes a long moment to let this settle, and then she finally says, "No. No. I know. I get it. I feel that way too."

"Really? You do?" I'm genuinely surprised. "Why? Your life has been totally terrible."

She nods and gets a terse smile. "Thanks." She pats my shoulder.

"You're welcome. I'm super helpful. Everybody—"

"Yeah, everybody says so, I know." (I guess I do say it a lot. Huh. I may just let her start finishing it for me. We can make it a bit.) She goes on, "I saw Caroline and Diane today when I was picking up my stuff."

"Oh, yeah? Did, um"—I can't remember if the one I saw with the Christmas tree was Caroline or Diane. Shit— "either of them say anything about running into me the other day?"

"No. Why? Did you?"

"Yeah. I was kind of a dick to whichever one it was because you had just left and I was kind of freaking out."

"Oh. May have been Diane. She seemed extra annoyed with me."

"Yes! Diane. Pretty sure it was Diane. Unless it was Caroline. Anyway. Continue."

"Just..." She pauses for a while. "I'm... out. I guess. You know? Like, I'm moving on and they're still where they were."

I nod. I understand what she's feeling. I really do. "Yeah. Yeah. I get that," I say, stroking her cheek. "What do you want to do?"

"I dunno. Help them somehow. I guess?"

Now it's her turn to get sullen and self-retreating. We're a real barrel of monkeys. "What's up?"

"What am I gonna do, Ty?" She turns to face me. I move a strand of half-wet hair from her face.

"About what, angel?"

"With my life? I mean, I didn't really think much past the Carlos stuff. What's next?"

"Um, I... dunno. We hang out? Have sex? Travel around and shit? Get into adventures? Solve problems wherever we land? Like Bonnie and Clyde. Only not robbing banks but being helpful to people and shit. That sound fun at all?" I flash my toothiest grin. I know I'm super charming. I don't care if anybody says so.

She lets out a huge sigh. "Dude, I'm not just gonna live off you."

"Why not? Evan lives off Robert and he says it's the bomb."

"Yeah, but Evan has a job. No, not a job, a *calling*. He's doing the thing he's always loved and always wanted to do. I don't have that."

I consider this for a moment. That's tough. She's right. I've always known what I wanted. So did Evan. And Scotty, and... yeah. That's tough.

"Want to buy another drone?" I ask.

"Fuck a drone. That was a ridiculous idea. I don't know what the fuck I was thinking."

"Oh. Cool. Because I wasn't gonna say anything, but—" She shoots me a look that is simultaneously terrifying and... Nope. That's it. It's just terrifying. "Sorry. Continue."

"But I have to figure something out." She swirls her finger in the tub, letting her head fall back to rest on my chest.

"OK. Awesome. Well, then tomorrow let's talk about what I'm gonna say to my dad, figure out what you're gonna do with the rest of your life, and maybe see if we can get me a shave and a haircut. Deal?"

"Deal," she says, leaning in to give me a kiss on my chest. It feels like, if she does that enough times in our life together, she might...*might*...actually be able to heal my scars.

And then, suddenly, a cold chill races down my spine. I can't describe it, but it's that thing that people get when they joke that someone's walking over their grave, or whatever. A shock to my system that makes the hairs on my arm stand on end.

I don't know why it's happening or where it came from, but I look around a little just to make sure... I don't know what. I just do it. It's a sense of dread. Foreboding.

Shit. My guess would be that it's probably my subconscious cautioning me not to get too comfy. Because my subconscious probably can't believe that everything's as good as it is, given how FUBAR shit has been for so long.

I decide not to think about it too much and instead, I lift Maddie's chin up, bringing her mouth to mine and give her a long kiss. As our lips separate, she laughs and shakes her head.

"Wow. Deal with your dad, figure out my life, get you a haircut and shave. That's gonna be a full day."

"I know! Two of those things are gonna be really friggin' tough."

"Yeah." She sighs.

"Fortunately, sorting out your existence should only take a minute."

New-look Tyler Morgan can still be a smart-ass, I decide.

CHAPTER SIX

MADDIE

December 28th
Three Days Until New Year's Eve

"You want some tea?" Raven asks. We're sitting in her kitchen—well, I'm sitting at the small wooden table up against the windows that overlook her backyard and she's in the kitchen holding a tea pot under the tap, filling it with water.

I reached out this morning to see if Raven was available for a bit, right after we made Tyler's hair appointment with Rodney. I don't know what it is about seeing Raven that makes me feel like it's the right first step in... figuring out what my next step is going to be, but it is how it feels. Call it a hunch, call it intuition, call it having no fucking clue how to start centering myself and throwing a dart at the dart board. They're all probably the same thing.

"Yeah, sure," I say, nervously glancing at Brandon, who is sitting across the table from me just staring. At me, not Raven. There's one of those triple-tiered serving platter things between us, so he's partially obstructed by Christmas cookies and shit, but still, his gaze is... intense.

"So," I say, looking at him.

"OK, I guess," he answers. I've decided he's some kind of freaky mind-reader because he does that every time I open my mouth. Answers questions I never asked. But he's always right. Like... he knows things.

"What'd you guys do for Christmas?" Raven calls out from the other side of the kitchen island.

"Shit." I laugh. "You really don't want to know."

"OK," Raven says, wiping her hands on her apron as she walks up behind Brandon, places her hands on his shoulders, and leans down to bite the outer edge of his ear.

I cock my head at them like a confused dog. "You guys..."

"Yup," Brandon says.

"Uh-huh," I say back, just staring at the two of them. Raven plops down into the chair next to me. It's not a table chair, per se. It's like... an accent chair. All comfortable with throw pillows and thick arm rests. Kinda homey and classy at the same time.

Which, surprisingly, is kind of a metaphor for Raven right now as well. She's baking today, hence the apron. And from the look of the triple-tier tray of cookies, she does this a lot. But under the apron—which is white cotton with ruffled edges and has a vintage fifties cherry pattern on it—she's wearing a long white dress that flows around her legs like ethereal smoke when she walks.

"Who *are* you guys?" I ask.

Raven laughs, grabs a Christmas cookie off the tray, and takes a bite. "Just people," she says.

"Right. So..." I look at Brandon, waiting to see if he'll answer this question before I ask it as well, but he doesn't. Probably because he already knows it was a question for Raven, not him.

Freaky mind-reader.

"So what are you up to these days?"

"Well." Raven sighs. "Dealing with insurance shit, mostly. I hired an architect to give me the lowdown on what it's gonna take to rebuild Pete's and—"

"Did he leave it to you?" I interrupt. "Like in his will?"

"Not exactly," Raven says, smiling as she chews her cookie. "We were partners."

"Partners?"

"I was the silent kind. I mean, as far as the stripper shit went I was just the manager. But I took lead on the good deeds department."

"Good deeds department?" I ask, thoroughly confused.

"Yeah." She sighs. "Well, you wouldn't." Know about that, she means. Obviously, Brandon's freaky mind-reading skills have rubbed off on her. "Because we didn't advertise or anything. But we had feelers out."

"I'm sorry, what the fuck are you talking about?"

Raven laughs again. "Tell me something, Maddie."

"Sure," I say. "What?"

"How did you find us?"

"You mean Pete's?"

"Yeah, how did you know to come ask for a job at Pete's?"

"I just kinda..." I was gonna say went in there, but that wasn't how it happened at all, was it? "I came across a flyer one day. When I was shopping for a drone."

"Yeah, I'd heard you talk about that stupid drone before. What was the deal with that?"

I wave a hand in the air. "Just one of my harebrained ideas."

"OK, so you found a flyer. What did it look like?"

I shrug. "It was red paper with black writing. Had an illustration of a girl swinging around a pole wearing a devil costume."

Raven lifts one eyebrow. She and Brandon share a look.

"What?" I ask. "What's that look for?"

"Go on," Raven says. "Finish the story."

Something is happening here, I'm just not sure what. "Well," I continue. "It had dollar signs on it and had something like 'Make Quick Cash' printed at the top."

"So you picked it up at this... drone store..."

"Yes," I say.

"And what? You needed cash? For that Carlos shit?"

"Yeah." I shrug. "So I went in and applied. And you know the rest because you're the one who interviewed me."

"You were wearing white that day," she says.

"Was I?"

"Yes, you were. White shorts, white tank top, and white wedge shoes. Which is why I hired you."

"How do you remember that? And what do you mean, that's why you hired me?"

She sticks the rest of her cookie into her mouth and brushes crumbs off her hands as she chews. Then she smiles and says, "Pete's was just a strip club to most people. But underneath he and I had a little... thing going."

"What kind of thing?" I ask. "And what the fuck did you mean you had feelers out?"

But the tea pot starts screaming and she jumps up, saying, "One sec. Hold that thought," as she goes back behind the kitchen island and starts pouring tea.

I glance at Brandon just as he takes two cookies off the tray, places them on the table in front of him, and then smiles as he lifts one up to his mouth and takes a bite.

These people really have a thing for cookies.

Raven returns with our tea on a serving platter. She places a mug in front of me, in front of Brandon, and in front of her place at the table, and sets down a sugar bowl filled with light brown cubes, a small ceramic pitcher of milk, and a little container of honey with one of those cute wooden dippers.

I take a bunch of sugar cubes, add a splash of milk, and they both opt for honey and no milk.

"Mmmm," I say, taking a sip of tea. "Thanks, I needed this."

"OK," Raven says, settling back in her chair and bringing her legs up so her knees are in front of her. "So I met Pete a while back. Before Carolina died. They were running the strip club already and I was working there. Pretty much just doing what you were doing. Being defensive and haughty."

"Hey." I laugh.

"Truth, Scarlett, truth."

"Whatever."

"I was about your age too, maybe a little younger. I'd just had a baby, so I was kinda desperate."

"Wait," I say, looking around. "You have a kid?"

"I did," Raven says. She looks sad all of a sudden. "I gave her up for adoption."

"Oh," I say. Jesus Christ. I have no clue who she is right now. I mean, I'd assumed I knew who she was, but clearly I have no idea.

"I got pregnant and my boyfriend left me. I had a job, but it was just waitressing. The two of us together could afford the place we rented, but me alone?" She laughs. "Not enough tips to take care of that. So I was gonna get an abortion and just erase that part of my life completely, but dumbass me wandered into one of those health clinics run by nuns and shit, so they talked me out of it."

"Oh, that sucks," I say.

"No," she says. "Not really. I mean yeah, I was really pissed off when I found out they only ran that free clinic to like, talk bitches like me out of getting abortions. Like... I got rage-y with those do-gooders and started screaming and yelling. But they gave me a home. Sent me to live with this couple who were looking to adopt, who took care of me, and sent me to therapy, and bought me an insurance plan so I could get prenatal care, and gave me money for school. Shit like that. And at first it was like... yeah, I want all your free shit, but you can't have my baby. I mean, it felt like a transaction, ya know? And I was all emotional like pregnant women get, and well, it was not pretty. But in the end I did decide to let them adopt her, and they said we could have one of those open adoptions, ya know? Like, I could remain a part of her life if I wanted. They were actually cool about it. The only catch was that I'd have to move out because that would make it all too weird."

I try to picture her. Young. Desperate. Sad.

"And it was... well, a little bit harder than it sounded to pack my shit after I gave birth and just leave her behind."

"I can't even imagine."

She shrugs. "It was the right thing to do. I wasn't strung out or any bullshit like that, but my history was checkered with so many bad decisions. I just... I just pictured her life without me versus her life *with* me and... decided she was better off, ya know?"

"So you left her behind?"

"Yup. I took that money they gave me for school, got on a plane to Vegas, and used that money to rent a place and start again."

"As a stripper at Pete's?"

She nods. "I stumbled in there one afternoon after finding a flyer. A red one with black writing and an illustration of a devil swinging around a pole."

I am actually incapable of words right now. My mind is racing trying to fit all the pieces together, but I can't. They make no sense.

"I was drawn to those dollar signs too," she says, looking over at Brandon with a smile.

I glance at him just in time to see him smile back. Well, sorta. His lips kinda tilt upwards a tiny bit.

"And that's how it started."

"But... but what does that have to do with—?"

"I came into the club holding that red flyer and Pete took one look at it and said, 'Not hiring.' But Carolina was there, and she took it from my hand and gave me another one—this one was white and had all the same stuff on it. Same text, same dollar signs, same picture—but with one change. There was an angel swinging around the pole, not a devil. And she said, 'I think you meant to bring this one, right, dear?' And I said, What?' And then she winked at me, winked at Pete, and he said, 'You can start tomorrow at five AM. You've got morning shifts.'"

Things aren't coming full circle. I have nothing to say about this story except... "What the fuck?"

Raven smiles at Brandon again. Like there's something underneath that explains everything and I'm not privy to it. Then she refocuses her attention on me. "Carolina had this deal with a local church. Desperate girls would come to them—kinda like I went to those church people when I was pregnant—and sometimes they'd send them to Pete's."

"I'm sorry, wait. What? The *church* would send them to *Pete's*?"

"Well, not as a matter of course, obviously. Jesus. But if, after talking with them and assessing where they were at and what they needed and so forth, and especially if they had any experience on the street or dancing or whatever, it was the one place where they could work safely. Legally. Make money to feed their kids and pay rent. And not have to be walking the Strip selling their bodies or God knows what."

"That sounds like a very progressive church," I muse.

"Judge not lest ye be there, Scarlett."

Touché.

"So you had the red flyer," I say.

"And so did you," she responds.

"Yeah."

"And when Carolina got sick... well, she was trying to make sure she left something behind. Pete was on board with the good deeds but didn't want to run it. Desperate girls don't relate well to a man, he said. By the time they got to the point where they came to him, men had usually been the problem and they needed a woman who understood. And I dunno, Carolina saw something in me, I guess. Potential. Or some business sense, or hell, maybe it was just my sadness after leaving my baby girl behind so she could have a better life than I did." She shrugs. "And she gave me her half of the business, with the stipulation that I could never sell it. It was mine, but only as long as I stuck around to help others."

"So that's why you're still there. Or were still there before it burned down."

· "No," Raven says. "That's not why. Pete signed over my half after Carolina died. Said it was my life, my choice, and I was a grown woman who could make her own decisions. I stayed because... well, I like being the angel in disguise. I like being who I am. I like seeing the girls come in and change themselves. Change their lives. I like guiding them. Playing big sister or whatever. It... it just fulfills me."

I feel sick all of a sudden. Not because of Raven choosing to be a stripper for all these years, but because I was so, so, so wrong about her.

"You wanna see a picture?" Raven asks, pushing her chair back from the table and standing up before I can even answer. "Give me one sec."

I look over at Brandon. He doesn't smile. Just places one finger on top of the remaining cookie sitting in front of him and slides it across the table at me.

It's an angel. Decorated with a white frosting dress with pale blue flowers as accents. She's got a gold halo over her head.

This time when I look back at Brandon, he *is* smiling. He says, "They're good."

I pick it up and take a bite. It's sweet and reminds me of Christmas when I was a kid and my mom used to bake cookies too. Reminds me of happy times, before I fell down the mountain and needed to claw my way back up.

Raven comes back holding a thick photo album, which she opens and places on the table in front of me. She flips to the last page and points to a teenage girl. Black hair, dark eyes, wearing a swim suit and holding up a gold medal.

"She's on the US team for the next summer Olympics," Raven says, her voice cracking with... what? Sadness? Regret? Loss?

No. Pride.

"This was the previous year's world championships. She actually won three gold medals. This picture was taken just after her first win." Raven laughs unexpectedly. "She thought that was the best moment of her life. She had no idea what was coming next."

I just stare at the girl. But then Raven sits down, scoots her chair closer to me, and flips the album back to the first page. There's a picture of her—young, smiling, looking very tired as she holds a brand-new baby in her arms.

"Does she know you?" I ask, suddenly heartbroken and happy at the same time.

"No," Raven says softly. "When I left I told her parents, 'Don't mention me. If she asks, you can tell her, but not until she asks.' And so they send pictures every month. She's so fucking interesting, Maddie. So smart, and pretty, and just... spectacular. Every month I'm just blown away at what she's doing with her life. And when I think back to all those choices I made—to keep her, to give her away, and then to walk away—well, when I see this, when I see how much I'd have stifled her full potential by being selfish ..." She sniffs back the sadness, lifts her head to look me in the eyes, and says, "I did all the right things. Made all the right decisions. And I wouldn't take any of it back. I have no regrets at all."

We spend the next hour looking at every single page in that photo album. And then Raven kicks me out. Says she's having a party tonight and needs to get ready.

Brandon walks me to the door, holds it open for me, and says, "Take an angel with you." And then he hands me a bag of cookies, which I had no idea he was holding, and as soon as I take it, he closes the door.

I think about everything the whole way back to Evan and Robert's house.

All my bad decisions led me here. To this moment. To that interaction in Raven's kitchen.

Maybe she's right. Maybe all our mistakes add up to something bigger. Maybe all the bad decisions were just good ones in disguise.

I have been a failure for seven years. But I learned something from each one. I fell down, but I got back up. Stronger than I was. Better than I was.

And now I need to make the past mean something.

I don't know what that looks like. I don't know how I'm gonna do it, but I believe I can. I am nothing if not a fighter.

So I decide to embrace Scarlett. I decide to accept that I strayed, receive the gift of wisdom, and believe in who I am. Both the good *and* the evil.

I decide, after all, I can be just like Raven.

I decide I can be the angel in disguise.

CHAPTER SEVEN

TYLER

"Don't be silly. I was glad you called. Come on in. Tea?" That's Rodney. Maddie just thanked him for seeing us on short notice. His salon is fucking beautiful. Wood, and steel, and fine artwork hanging everywhere. As I understand it, he's THE guy all the hot-shit Vegas celebrities go to. I have a feeling this whole thing is gonna run me close to four figures, which is fine, just weird since I think the last time I got a haircut I spent like three hundred rupees (about five bucks) and traded a bowl of rice that had been handed to me for some reason. (Lady just shoved it at me and said, "Please. You. You." I figured that if I was looking so rough that she was forcing food on me, it must have been time for a trim.)

"Oh, no, I'm all tea'd up for today, thanks," says Maddie.

"Tyler?" asks Rodney.

"Um, sure. You got any rooibos?"

"What kind of hair salon do you think I'm running? Of course I do!" He nods to a young guy in a sweatshirt and jeans that are so tight they look like they came from Maddie's dresser, and Skinny Jeans heads over to where there's this elaborate, Japanese-looking tea station set up.

I suppose the tea service is gonna be an extra hundo, at least. Jesus.

But it's not the money. Not really. It's that with everything that's on my mind right now, blowing fat stacks on something as vanity-driven as a fuckin' shave and haircut feels insanely wasteful. But then I remind myself that I'm not doing this for me. I'm doing it because it will make Maddie happy. And that's a good enough reason for me to do pretty much anything.

"So! What are we doing with all this?" Rodney starts running his hands through my hair and stroking my beard. Which I don't mind necessarily. I'm not a huge fan of people poking and prodding at me uninvited, but it's his job and whatnot. Like when I get a physical, it's the doctor's job to grab my balls and shit, so I let 'em. It's just not the way I normally like to have my balls squeezed. Now, if Rodney grabs my balls, then that will be something that he and I will have to talk about.

I'll at least make him buy me dinner.

"Um... Mads? What're we doing?" I ask. Because I don't fuckin' know.

She walks me over and plops me down in the haircutting chair (I guess that's what it's called) facing a mirror and stands behind me with Rodney. "So, all this?" She rubs both hands down the sides of my cheeks, tracing my beard with her palms. And I'm getting hard. Oh, fuck. (Well, hell. The heart wants what it wants. So do my big, swollen nuts.) "Gone," she continues.

"All of it? Off?" he confirms.

She nods. "And then this?" She has her hands in my head hair now. "Let's just bring it up about this much..." She pulls my hair down in the front so that it's covering my face and then puts her index and middle finger, like scissors, around a chunk of it.

"Oh, really?" he says. "Because I was thinking we could go *this* much." He does the same thing, only a little higher up. They continue this conversation, both of them with their hands in my hair now.

"You think?" she asks.

"Definitely," he says. "You know, less Chris Hemsworth in *Thor* and more Chris Hemsworth on the cover of *Vanity Fair*. See?"

I assume he's holding up a copy of *Vanity Fair*, because Maddie goes, "Oh, my God. Yes. Yes. That is hot." I can't see what they're seeing because my hair is now all rumpled, having been man- and lady-handled, and is hanging in front of my face completely. I kind of feel like Cousin Itt from *The Addams Family*.

My tea is now ready.

Skinny Jeans hands it to me in a heavy, ceramic mug with no handle. I part my hair enough to bring the cup to my lips. Holy shit, that's the best fucking cup of goddamn rooibos tea I've ever had. Nice work, Skinny Jeans.

"OK! Let's get started!" exclaims Rodney, pulling my hair back from my face, snatching up a pair of scissors, grabbing my beard, and unceremoniously cutting off a huge chunk of it.

"AHHH!" I scream.

Both Maddie and Rodney jump back. "What? What happened?" Maddie yells.

"Nothing. Sorry. I was just fucking around. Continue."

Maddie rolls her eyes, and Rodney lets out a huge breath and slaps me on the shoulder. "You are bad!"

"You have no idea," says Maddie.

"OK. You"—Rodney addresses Mads—"out. Go. No distractions. I know how to deal with this. I've worked with children before." Good old Rodney's got my number, all right.

"Yeah? I should leave?" she asks, hesitantly.

I get it. I don't want her to go either. Not because of the fucking haircut. Despite all evidence to the contrary, I'm not actually five. It's just that being apart seems... hard. I don't like not being near her and I'm pretty sure she feels the same way. And even though it's just some hair being taken off my face and head, it's more than that.

This is the only way she's seen me since I left twelve years ago. This version of me is who she has fallen in love with. If she goes away and comes back, a whole new person will be sitting here to greet her. Someone who looks like she probably remembers. And that may be a good thing. It may be an awful thing. No way to know. And only one way to find out.

"Hey," I say, extending my hand out to her. She takes it. "I'll see you in a little bit."

She doesn't seem sure. She rocks back and forth like she doesn't want to let go of my grip. And then Rodney says, "Oh! Shit. I left my good shaving brush in the back. I'll go get it." He turns and heads to the back, shooing Skinny Jeans out along with him. Good dude.

Once they're gone, I fan my hair back away from my face and turn the chair to face Mads. "Hey, kitten, I'm just getting a haircut and a shave. But it's me. I'll still be here."

"I know," she says. "I know. It's stupid, but..."

"No, it ain't stupid," I say. "Shit, kid, after everything we've been through in the last couple months, it's not unreasonable for you to think you could come back to find Lady Gaga sitting here waiting for you."

She squints at me. Peers hard into my eyes. "Are you Lady Gaga?"

I consider. "Not sure. Don't think so."

"Because that wouldn't be the worst. Gaga's fucking hot." She smiles. I smile back and squeeze her hand tighter.

"I'll be here. I ain't going nowhere. Bank on that shit."

She nods and squeezes my hand back. Then she grabs up her bag, heads to the door, and throws me one last look over her shoulder. I wink and then make an over-exaggerated series of flamboyant, Vegas magician gestures all around my beard and head, and she smirks, laughs only through her nose, and then walks out, letting the door fall shut behind her.

I swivel the chair back around to look at myself in the mirror again. She's not the only one who's a little worried. Shit, I don't know if I'll even recognize my own damn self anymore. It's been probably seven or eight years since I saw my face unobscured by this jungle of protective overgrowth. Because for all the shit I've talked about being lazy or not caring – which is not completely untrue – an even truer reason that I've allowed myself to look this way is that it keeps people at a distance. It creates a barrier. It hides me.

So. Time to come out of the darkness and into the light.

Rodney pokes his head around the corner to see if Maddie's gone. "Found it!" he says, holding up a swanky-looking shaving brush with a silver handle. "OK! Let's do this," he exclaims, walking over to me.

He grabs a hot towel from a towel steamer and goes to wrap it around my beard and eyes. Just before he puts it on me, I reach out and grab his arm, stopping him. "Rodney... Be gentle," I implore, with an over-exaggerated need in my voice.

"Oh, honey," he says, "Rodney's got you, baby."

And as he leans the chair back and wraps the warm, damp towel around my eyes, I choose not to think about how goddamn vulnerable this whole thing could make a person feel.

CHAPTER EIGHT

MADDIE

Outside I feel kinda lost. I mean, I know where I am. I just feel like I don't *know* where I am. My heart is jumping a little. And I suddenly realize I can hear it.

Is that normal?

I'm not sure what's going on but I stop at a street corner and lean against a lamppost, taking a moment to just be still. Think. I'm just—

"You OK?"

"What??" I snap my head and look around but no one's there.

Well, there's lots of people but none of them are looking or talking to me.

Am I hearing things?

I'm sure there's like a dozen rational explanations for how I feel right now, it's just the frontrunner is leaning towards... what?

God, I don't know what's wrong with me. I just feel like I need to look around. Check my back and see if anyone is there.

Which is stupid. Leftover side effects of the whole drug-lord thing down in Mexico, that's all. Maybe it was my devil talking to me?

But I check my shoulders and nope. That asshole has taken the day off.

"Jesus Christ," I whisper, crossing the street. "You are insane, Maddie." Not because I'm hearing things. Because I actually looked for the devil on my shoulder.

I keep walking, unsure of what to do with myself while Tyler...

Unsure about anything, really. How does that happen? One second you're cool with everything in your life and the next second you're not?

Is it because I'm not seeing what's happening with Tyler?

The farther I get away from the salon, the more uneasy I become. My heart is definitely thumping now. I can feel the blood pumping through my body like a building sense of panic.

So I do what I do. The only thing I know how to do. The only thing I *can* do.

I pretend it's not happening. I smile. I feel the wind on my face. I walk.

I. Keep. Going.

And that's when I realize this is the same direction I was walking on Halloween. That Pete's is just a few blocks away.

My feet suddenly have a destination and this, for whatever reason, makes all the difference. I inhale, exhale, and then the thumping is gone. The sense of uneasiness fades with each step I take towards Pete's. And by the time I get to the burned-down rubble where I used to work, I am calm.

Which also makes no sense at all. Or else it absolutely does.

"Do you know what happened?"

I startle again, but this time when I glance over to my shoulder, I find a young woman dressed like a hooker, looking like she's been awake for way too long. "Bad shit," I sigh in reply.

She's smoking a cigarette, which she flicks, and drags, and flicks again. Eyes taking in the scene. She says, "Yeah. I tried to get a job here."

She's obviously strung out and I wonder if there's any chance Pete would have ever hired this woman. Probably not. "I just pulled an all-nighter." I think she says it by way of explaining her strung out looking state. Because it comes out slightly defensive.

"Yeah?" I reply back.

"Yep," she says, dragging her tired eyes up to mine to stare dead into them. Then she adds, "...I'm leaving today."

"Yeah?" I ask. "Where ya going?"

"Home," she says. Like everyone knows where home is.

"I needed the bus fare, so I worked all night. But before I made up my mind to leave, I was thinking about working here. I heard the guy was a good guy. The owner. What was his name?"

After a pause, I say, "Pete."

"Yeah. Heard he was a good guy."

"He was," I say.

"I interviewed a few months ago but he turned me down. Said I should get clean."

I nod. "And did you?"

She scowls at me. Because I think she feels like it was a judgement. Maybe it was. I don't want it to be, but maybe it was. "I'm better than I was before," she says.

I nod. I get it. I mean, she looks like shit now but bad is a bottomless pit, right? "I worked here," I say.

When I glance over at her, she's already looking at me. "I know," she says. "Feel like I've seen you around."

"Oh," I say. Weird. The realization that people you don't notice can notice you. "It was a...good place," I say. Because it was. "He *was* a good guy."

She nods. Sighs. Drags on her cigarette. Drops it to the ground and stomps it out with her hooker shoe. "I didn't really know him. Couple times he saw me hanging around and gave me some breakfast. Before..." She waves her hand in the air, like 'before' encompasses a whole load of baggage. "But yeah, I came out of the hospital a few days ago and I swung by here. To tell him I was serious. That I was gonna get clean and come back in a few months to get that job and quit all this shit. But..."

She doesn't finish. Doesn't need to.

But it was gone. Plan A was a non-starter.

"You look good," she says.

"I do?"

She nods. "Yeah. I mean, Like I say, I've seen you around and yeah, you look better. I was standing over there," she says, pointing to a street corner. "Just got dropped off from my last call ever." Which makes her smile. Almost laugh. "And there you were. And I thought to myself, *Damn. She looks good.* And then I was thinking... like, you give me hope."

"I do? How? Why, I mean."

She shrugs, "I saw how you were a couple months back. You had this crazy look in your eyes all the time. Which, and I'm not judging, OK?" She makes a special point of letting me know that she's not judging *me*. "But it came off as kinda desperate. And I used to think... I'm not the only one. But then it seemed like you got better. And it was bugging me."

I don't actually know what to say to her. I'm just... stunned that this woman I never met seems to have so much of her...time...invested in me.

"It bugged me that you were changing, I guess. Maybe I was jealous?" She smiles at me. An embarrassed smile. "I'm not giving up though. I'm one of those tough bitches, ya know?"

Which makes *me* smile. Kinda big. "I do know."

"I just keep climbing. I never look down, either. That's pointless. I just keep my head up and climb. It's all you can do. Give up or keep climbing. And I'm just not a quitter. I wish I was, it'd be easier. But I'm not. Do you know what I'm talking about?"

I just nod, dumbly. I'm speechless.

"So... it's hard. But I got my bus fare." She looks down at her small purse and pats it. "Worked all night to get it and now I'm leaving."

I want to say all kinds of things. Stupid motivational things that mean nothing unless you're saying them to yourself. Things like, *Hang in there. It gets better.*

But I don't. And she turns to leave.

I don't want her to leave, I realize. So I say, "Hey?"

She stops walking and looks over her shoulder at me. "Yeah?"

"You need anything? Money? A ride? I can call you a car or get you a taxi."

She shakes her head. "Thanks, but no. I'm good. I'm really good."

And then she turns and walks away. Disappears from view as if she was never really there. Like a figment of my imagination. She just fades into the crowd.

It's only then that I realize there's loads of people around. People who like... faded into the background while we were talking. That life goes on, no matter what. The world never stops turning. The sun keeps rising, the night always comes, and then the light takes its place.

Every twenty-four hours there's a new opportunity for a fresh start.

That girl. We are the same person, she and I.

I hope she makes it.

I wish I could help her.

I will help her.

Maybe not her, specifically. But people like her.

People like us. People who fuck up and keep going.

People who never give up.

CHAPTER NINE

TYLER

Each snip of the scissors cutting off strands of my hair is like letting go of something I've been holding onto too tightly. Not memories. Those will, I imagine, stay with me forever. Or at least until I get old and senile. Which is a weird thing to ponder, considering that I never thought I'd live past twenty-five. Every day since then has been unexpected.

But it's the *feelings* that seem like they're drifting to the ground with each new cut.

Snip.

Mom dying. What that felt like. Falling to the floor.

Snip.

The explosion. The one that killed Nadir. Floating to the ground.

Snip.

Getting the word that Scotty was gone. The shock. The loss. The retreat from everyone and everything. Being carried to the earth with the former extensions of me.

Snip.

Rodney's not talking now. He was at first. Very chatty. Like, I suppose people expect from their barber (or *stylist*, I guess). First thing he asked was, "So did you guys have a good Christmas?"

That's one of those things people say, right? Like, "Did you have a happy birthday?" Or, if you went to a party or something, "Did you have a nice time?" Or, like if you're married or whatever, "How's John?" And shit like that.

And nobody ever expects or plans for the answers to be, "No, my birthday was shitty." Or, "The party sucked. I got food poisoning." Or, "John left me. He ran off with the pool boy."

It's not really people's fault, I guess. We're all just taught to be polite and to make conversation and shit. It's an easy way to sound like you care. Because we're all supposed to care about each other. Which isn't the same thing as caring *for* each other, of course. Almost nobody wants to do that.

I'm only thinking about all this shit now because of all the other shit I'm also thinking about now. About how I can, like, make a difference. Or help people. Or whatever the hell I'm planning on doing. Because I don't really give a shit about being "nice." Anybody can be "nice." I think what I want to be is... kind. Which is a different thing altogether.

Which is why, even though my impulse was to answer Rodney's question with, "No. Not really. Went down to Mexico. Got into a gun fight with a drug jefe and watched some dudes get killed," I chose to *consider* him, and the fact that he's just trying to get through his day like everybody else, and said, "Not bad. You?"

Which was great, because then he went off on a long soliloquy about his boyfriend Thomas (the one I kept referring to in my head as Bow Tie at Thanksgiving) and how Christmas is hard for Thomas because of the rough time he had growing up, and yadda, yadda, yadda. And what was weird was that I found myself really paying attention. Not going, "Uh-huh, oh, really? Wow!" and all that shit, but genuinely *hearing* what he was saying. Like, my mind didn't wander off to random lines of dialogue from *Jaws* or what-the-fuck-ever. I stayed completely invested in the shit he was telling me and was just... there.

When he realized how long he had been going on he said, "Jesus. I'm sorry. You don't want to hear all my bullshit."

"No, no," I told him. "It's fine. Go on."

And then he did. And when he finally got to the end and had kind of talked himself out he said, "Thanks for listening."

And I said, "No problem." Because it really wasn't. Which was... different. For me.

But now he's all business. He's turned the chair so that my back is facing the mirror. I think he's doing it partially so that he has the space to really maneuver around and assess and decide his next move from all angles, and partially because I think he's kind of excited for me to get "the big reveal."

It's funny to watch him. He looks the way artists do when they're standing back from their canvases trying to determine what else a painting needs. He narrows his eyes. He steps forward. Then he steps back and shakes his head. I'm just sitting here watching the whole thing, trying to not fall asleep. Which is not because I'm tired. It's actually just one of those things that happens when you have bundled energy and no place to put it.

And then, just as Rodney starts nodding his head like he's happy with what he's done, on cue, Maddie walks back in.

When she sees me, she puts her hand to her mouth reflexively. Rodney snaps his head to see her standing there. "Wait, wait, wait, I'm not sure I'm finished!" He steps toward me again, places the scissors near my temple, but once again decides better of it and steps back, saying, "OK, no. I am."

He crosses his arms and rolls his neck around like he just got finished doing a heart transplant or something. And now Maddie walks over to stand beside him, her hand still over her mouth. I can feel my eyes widening in the way that precedes the question, "What? What the fuck is it?" But I don't actually ask the question, because I know what the fuck it is. Or I can imagine.

Rodney lets out a long sigh through his nostrils and then says, "So?"

Maddie shakes her head a bit, lowering her hand slowly from her face. Then the head shake turns into a nod. "Yeah," she says. "Yeah." Then she says it a third time. "Yeah."

"Gotta be real," I say. "Freaking me out a *little* bit, gang."

Skinny Jeans now turns the corner from the back, carrying a tray with hair shit on it—razors, scissors, product, all that stuff. And when he sees me, the tray crashes to the ground, he puts both hands over his heart, and says, "Oh, my heavenly fuck."

Both Maddie and Rodney jump at the sound of the crashing tray and then they grab each other around the biceps, clutching tightly, as they turn back to me.

"More freaked out now, FYI," I mention. "Guys, what the fuck? Look like you're walking through the jungle and just ran up on a lion."

Maddie approaches me tentatively, both hands pressed together, as if in prayer, her fingertips resting against her lips. She looks down at the unreal amount of hair on the floor. It's like somebody just sheared a small animal or something. I've still got on the apron thing that Rodney clipped around my neck, so my body is totally hidden and just my head is poking out. Maddie puts both her hands on the arms of the chair so that I'm now pinned down under the tarp that covers me. She stares at me. Finally, I say, "Hey."

Her eyes crinkle up and she says, "Hey."

She lifts her hand up and strokes my cheek. It feels weird. Her hand is actually touching my *face*. The skin that covers my bones. I think about my talk with Brandon in the park last week: His notion that a person is not made of the things they say, or the things they think, or even the things they do.

And he's right, of course.

What makes a person a person is something unidentifiable. It sure as hell isn't the skin we wear. I know that as well as anybody. The way a thing looks is like the least of what makes it it. Like the old Buddhist riddle goes, 'If you strip a rose of its petals and thorns and bud and all the rest of it, is it still a rose?'

Who knows?

But still. The skin we're in. That's what people see.

And what they see is how they recognize what's in front of them. And so, for the first time in a dozen years, I suppose Maddie recognizes somebody she used to see all the time, sitting in front of her once again. I wonder how that must feel. For the briefest of flashes, I have this jolt of anxiety that all the angry feelings she had, and all the resentment, will come pouring back over her. Because THIS is the guy she hated in her head. THIS is the guy who broke her heart and her spirit without even knowing he was doing it. THIS is the guy. So I need to know what she's feeling.

I ask her in the best way I know how.

"Do I look like Lady Gaga?"

She smiles and says, "Almost as good." And then she gives me a kiss.

Wow. Holy shit. The feeling of her lips on mine with nothing in between us? No dense shrubbery that she has to hack through to get to me waiting on the other side? It feels unreal. This is the first time a woman's lips have touched mine without impediment in... well. Probably my whole life, actually. Because the beard was only the physical manifestation of the barricades I had up.

And I can't even begin to imagine what it's going to feel like when my naked, hungry mouth gets to place itself on the rest of her body.

Rodney approaches cautiously and asks, "Wanna see yourself?"

"Guys, Jesus. I just got a fuckin' haircut. It's not like you performed plastic surgery."

"Oh, didn't I?" Rodney asks, arching his right eyebrow and then his left. (Fuckin' showoff.)

Maddie steps to the side. Rodney places his hands on the arms of the chair where hers were and spins it around. I look at them standing behind me in the mirror. They seem excited. Like when someone is unwrapping a present you gave them and you're simultaneously eager and nervous to see what they're going to think of it.

And then my eyes track away from them and settle on the image looking directly back at me in the mirror. A reflection of somebody that I wasn't even sure was there anymore.

A reflection.

Huh.

That word can mean a lot of things.

Reflection.

And on a deep inhale, I silently acknowledge it all.

Hey, dude. Long time.

CHAPTER TEN

MADDIE & TYLER

MADDIE

"What?" Tyler asks. He's looking over at me in the passenger seat. There's a little bit of traffic, so he's keeping one eye on the road, but the other one keeps drifting back to me. And I know I'm staring. But I can't stop. It's one thing to have *known* that it's Tyler I'm with. It's another thing to *see* him. The guy I knew before.

For the most part, anyway.

"Nothing. You just..." But I run out of words and instead lean across the front seat of the Tesla, grab his face, and kiss him on the mouth. He kisses me hard back and then there's some honking as the car swerves and Tyler jerks the wheel. I sit back in my seat but leave my hand on his leg. Right next to the erection he now has going. "Does that ever not happen?" I ask.

"What?" he responds. I gesture down at his crotch with a nod of my head. "Oh. Uh, with you? No. Not so far as I can tell. Why? Does it bug you?"

"God, no. No. I just... wondered."

"I mean, you can't kill it, but you can feed it what it needs, and it'll be satisfied for a while," he says on a grin.

"And so, in this metaphor, your dick is a...?"

"I dunno. Unkillable python?"

I smirk, pat his leg, and lie back in my seat again.

"Oh," he says. "That did it. You made him sleepy. He's going away. Night-night, buddy. We'll miss you."

Dork.

"Hey," he says. "I'm an asshole. I didn't ask. How was it this morning?"

"What? With Raven?"

"Yeah."

"OK. We had tea and cookies." I know what he's asking about, but he's not the only one who can be a smartass.

"Uh-huh. Super. And do you have your life all figured out now via tea and cookies with a stripper?"

"Yeah," I say. "Maybe."

He sits up a little straighter. "Really? Fuck, I was just fuckin' around. Do tell."

"Dunno. I mean, I don't have all the answers or whatever, but it did cause me to pivot my focus."

"How do you mean?"

I shrug. "Just, y'know, I was already on my way here, but... the stuff we talked about with not being a victim anymore, or not blaming the past. I think... I think what I really crystallized for myself this morning is that I just need to *embrace* everything I've done that seemed like a fucking terrible mistake, rather than turn my back on it. Does that make sense?"

He nods his head a couple of times and then glances over at me. "Intellectually," he says.

"Yeah. Harder to put into practice, I know, but shit, man... look at everything we've both been through. Hell, look what we went through just this fuckin' week! Neither one of us should be here, so, I mean, the fact that we are? We should look at ourselves as worthy. Because now, what I believe is..." I pause to consider what it is that I do believe. "I guess now what I'm thinking is... the biggest obstacle to doing something? Is not really and honestly believing in your heart that you can."

He's quiet for a second, then he says, "Musta been some cookie."

"It was pretty good." Then I say, "And look, it's not like I think you become an Olympic athlete by just *believing* in yourself—"

"Really? 'Cause I'm thinking of going for the shotput."

I ignore him. "But I am saying that people like you and me? People who have the *opportunity*? For people like us not to offer our hands...well, that's just a waste."

"'Us playing small does not serve the world,' as Nelson Mandela said?"

"Mandela didn't say that."

"What? Whatayou mean? He totally said it. He also said, uh, something like, 'Our deepest fear is not that we are inadequate. Our deepest fear is that we are powerful beyond measure,' or something."

"No." I sigh. "He didn't. Marianne Williamson said it in a book called *A Return To Love*."

"Really?"

I nod.

"Then why do people think Mandela said it?"

"I dunno. The internet?"

"How do you know he didn't?"

"The internet."

There's a moment and then he says, "Ain't that a bitch?"

"My point is," I say, trying to get this train back on the tracks, "that I think, on some level, the reason I've had such a hard time getting anywhere is because I was"—this part is hard to say out loud—"I was just thinking about me. And that's all well and good, but I'm not sure that's who I am. Or at least, it's not who I want to be. I don't want to be the person who thinks about Maddie—"

"I'll take that job."

"—I want to be the person who thinks about how Maddie can think outside of herself." I pause to consider how much I'm probably not making sense. "I dunno. I can't put it into words exactly. It's just more of a *feeling* I'm having."

"Well," he says. "Ask me, and—"

"I didn't."

"I know, but I don't care. Ask me, and I'd say that the feeling is the most important part. Because it means that the idea that was here"—he reaches over and touches me on my head—"is now something you feel here." He points at my stomach. "And that's where the urge to action comes from. You know, like when you're in battle. You're not thinking about how you're going to survive, you just survive. There's a reason it's called 'gut instinct.' The thinking part can come later."

For all his jokes and wisecracks, he can be a deeply soulful guy. It's always been that way. Which is why I've always loved him. He is, no question, the most complicated person I've ever met.

He points at my stomach again. "Or maybe it's just the cookies. How many did you have?"

Annnnnnd he's back.

Goddamn. He's so fucking handsome. It's a testament to how *sexy* he is that he could overcome how much the beard obscured how *handsome* he is. And now I get what he's talking about with his cock being at full mast all the time. Because I can feel myself starting to get wet just by looking at him. Holy shit.

And so I put my hand on his crotch and say, "No more talking about cookies. There's something else I'd rather have inside me."

TYLER

Oh, Christ, I so do not wanna crash this Tesla.

But she's making it hard. I mean that both ways!

"Um," I manage. "There's... Where...? Traffic," I think I might say.

"I dunno," she purrs out. "There's probably an alley somewhere." OK, so now she's fucking with me too? Who is this person? Devil woman! "Unless," she says, "you know, your ribs are too banged up still." And she pulls her hand off my already aching dick and runs it up under my shirt where she tickles at my ribs. Shit, I'm definitely gonna wreck this goddamn car.

And then, looking out the window, I realize where I am.

"Fuck it," I say, and jerk the car off Las Vegas Boulevard onto Aria Place.

"What are you doing?" she asks.

I don't say shit, just zip the Tesla down the ramp that leads to the valet stand of the Mandarin Oriental hotel parking, just below the Strip. I'm jumping out of the car before it even rolls to a stop. I think. Since it's all electric,

I can't hear an engine revving down. But my foot is dragging along the pavement. All good.

I throw it into park, hop out, and hand the key to Reggie, my favorite valet, saying, "Thanks, Reg." He clearly doesn't recognize me now, and must just assume I'm some rich dickhead who's getting familiar from having read his nametag. After the fire and everything, it's probably for the best that he doesn't know it's me. And I am a rich dickhead, so he wouldn't be all wrong.

"What are we—?" Maddie starts to ask, as I grab her hand and whip her inside through the revolving doors. I pull her with me over to the elevator that takes us up to the twenty-third-floor sky lobby and press the button repeatedly like pressing it more than once will make the elevator get here any faster. "What are we doing?" She gets the whole question out this time.

"It's a hotel. We're getting a room."

"Are you serious?"

"Serious as my cock is hard, sugar." And I wink. I probably look like a douchebag, but I hope it comes off as charming.

I also hope that when I get to the desk and give them my name and credit card it doesn't set off some kind of alarm in the system that sends a bunch of big, muscle-bound guys chasing after us. Mostly because with my ribs still a little tender, I dunno if I could take more than two at once. We'll find out shortly, I guess.

The elevator doors open, and I hustle us both inside, my hands on her ass and my tongue in her mouth the whole way up. There's nobody else in the car, but there are security cameras, and again, I'm going with the assumption that literal new-look Tyler isn't recognizable to anyone who may be watching.

The doors open and we step out into the sky-lobby. Looking to my left, I see that there's not too much of a line at reception, thankfully, so I scurry us over and a reception desk guy whose nametag says "Bryce" waves us to him with a, "May I help you?"

"Yeah, hi," I say, approaching my man Bryce. "Need a room. Please."

He looks at me with a half-confused expression. "OK. And the name on the reservation?"

"Uh, I don't have a reservation. I just need a room."

"Oh, um, I see," Bryce retorts as he starts tapping at his keyboard. "Well, um, it is the holidays, and New Year's is..." He goes on like that mumbling to himself.

"Yeah, I know. Bro, I just need a room." I smile at Maddie. She smiles back, coyly. And now I *really* need a room.

"Y'know, honestly," my main bro, Bryce, says. "We're pretty much fully committed." Which I know is bullshit. They always hold out a block of rooms for VIPs and shit.

"Are ya?" I ask. "Ya are? Even the Emperor Suite? How's that looking?"

Yeah. That grabs Bryce by the short and hairies, all right.

"Um." More typing. "Well... It *is* technically available. But it would be at our holiday premium rate."

"Cool," I say, pulling out my jumbled mess of loose bills, my one American Express Green card, and my license. "How much?" I slap the AmEx on the counter.

Bryce stares at me and says, "Ten thousand five hundred for the night."

"Sweet. Probably won't be here all night, but all good. Go ahead and run that bad boy," I tell him as I push the card his direction. I look back at Maddie with one finger raised in a "just bear with me, we're almost there" gesture.

After another blank look from Bryce and a "come on, my dude, let's get this show on the road" look from me, he says, "Can I have you fill this out?" and pushes a guest registration card my way as he swipes the AmEx.

I stare at the registration card for a moment, still pondering over how fucked I am if I put down that it's me, Tyler Morgan, the Mandarin Oriental Pyromaniac, checking in. I decide to just assume that he won't pay attention to the fact that the name on the credit card and the name on the registration don't match and I write Tyler Hudson. My middle name. Mom's maiden name.

And then I just make up a bullshit address. Whatever.

When Bryce pulls the receipt from the credit card machine for me to sign, he looks a little surprised, like homeboy can't believe shit went through. *Believe it, Bryce!* He slides it my way, saying, "You've stayed with us before?"

"Nah," I say as I sign, "just heard good things." I smile and wink as he hands me the key card in its little key card jacket.

He asks, "Can I have your bags brought—?" But I'm already on my way to the bank of elevators that will whisk us upstairs, Maddie's hand in mine.

We're not as lucky this time with nobody else being around. There's, like, a bevy of women, pretty solidly day-drunk, all gathered around, talking loudly. One of them goes, "No! YOU fucked him first!" And then they laugh. I like 'em. They seem fun.

But then they turn and see us, and I guess Maddie decides they're not as fun, because the look in her eyes changes suddenly and she steps in front of me and faces them down. One of them (the one who fucked him first, I suppose) shouts in Maddie's direction, "Yeah, girl, you better hold onto that!" And they all laugh again. (OK, yeah, I can see how they're not all that fun.) And then when the elevator dings, and the doors open, Maddie doesn't move as they all step on.

A different one holds the door for a second, and Maddie says, "No. We'll wait," with a sharp, confrontational tone in her voice. And, once again, they all laugh as the doors close. I can see Maddie's back kind of rising and falling now, the unexpected flash of anger she just showed toward these broads resting on her shoulders. And I can only think one thing about her protective and somewhat jealous display...

I can't wait to fuck each other's brains out in about five minutes.

MADDIE

It strikes me suddenly that I'm not the only one who will notice how fucking good Tyler looks now that he's all clean-shaven and you can really see that ridiculously fortunate bone structure he has. And I'm a little embarrassed about the fact that I just got all possessive and shit. I'm about to say something to that effect, either make a joke or play it off, but before I can, Tyler grabs me around the waist, pulls me to him and whispers, "That was so fucking hot," just as the doors to another elevator pop open.

He walks me backwards into the car and frantically pushes the "door close" button before anyone else can step in. He's got me pressed against the mirrored glass and his hands are between my denim-covered thighs, cupping my pussy. He kisses my neck and the feel of his lips, without any rough hair to brush and scratch against mine, feels so good that I can barely stand it. I didn't realize his kiss was so soft. The skin of his mouth feels new. Like, I was just starting to get accustomed to the way his kisses felt, and suddenly it's a whole new experience. New, but familiar. The same way it was when I met him.

It's how this whole moment feels. Back in the Mandarin where we were on Halloween when we found out who we are. A concept which, I realize in this moment, might be true in more ways than one. It's been barely two months since we turned each other's lives upside down. Except that's not quite fair. Or accurate. Our lives were already upside down. We've turned them back right side up. Yeah, we disrupted each other's worlds, but we did so in the most magnificent way. And it's starting to feel like that disruption is going to result in a life that actually feels... settled.

I realize that life with Tyler Morgan will never be boring. That much seems incredibly evident. But life is unpredictable no matter what we do to try to put rules in place to keep it from feeling that way. At least with Tyler the unpredictability doesn't seem scary. With him, as much as is possible, the unpredictability feels safe.

The doors to the elevator open and he backs out, pulling me with him. Not watching where we're going, we smack into the panel of buttons, lighting most of them up, and the doors start to close again. He throws his arm out to keep them from shutting and taking us to another floor and I start giggling. He does too. He nips at my lip with his teeth and when the doors spring open again, I bound past him, grabbing the key card from his hand, and run down the hall.

When I get to the end of the corridor, I realize that I don't know where I'm going and when I turn back, I see him standing at the other end of the hallway with his arms crossed. He clears his throat and thumbs at the door to his right, and I take off to where he's standing, throwing myself into him, wrapping my arms around his neck and kissing him on the mouth like I'm trying to break through him entirely.

We kiss for a few long moments, my hands running through his newly cut hair and down the sides of his newly shaved cheeks, and then he pulls the key card from me, spins me around, presses his hard cock against my ass, opens the door with the card, and propels us both inside. The second the door shuts behind us, he pulls off my shirt, walking me forward into the bedroom of this unbelievable suite. I see the whole of the Las Vegas Strip laid out at our feet. And an odd feeling lands on me. I don't feel special or spectacular. I don't feel fabulous or like it's a fantasy. And I don't even feel undeserving, unworthy, or guilty, which is something that I've definitely grown accustomed to in the past. I just feel... grateful.

I kick my shoes off as he pulls my pants and underwear down at the same time. I go to take my bra off, but he stops me, places my arms down by my sides, and snaps open the clasp himself. He slides the straps down my arms and it falls to the floor. As it does, I shiver a tiny bit. A small jolt of current runs through me.

"You cold?" he asks.

"No," I tell him on a whisper over my shoulder.

As I'm glancing back, I see him pulling off his own shirt and taking down his pants. I start to turn and face him, but he steps to me, flattening his cock between his belly and my ass, and holds my chin in his hand, nipping hard at my jawline with his mouth. I lift my hand up around the side of his head and press his cheek to mine. I rub my face back and forth along his. "You feel. So. Fucking. Good." I say.

"Yeah?" he hums back, his other hand cradling and massaging my ass.

"Yeah," I say. "Smooth. Soft. It feels so good."

"Well, then you're gonna love this," he says as he picks me up around the waist and literally tosses me face forward onto the massive bed. I shriek a little in surprise and delight and before I can say a word, he's behind me again, pulling me onto my hands and knees at the edge of the mattress. He drops down onto his knees on the floor behind me, puts both hands on my ass, spreads me open, and the next thing I know, his tongue is in my asshole. And all I can think is...

The razor may be my favorite invention of all time.

TYLER

Just like the beard was keeping me at a distance from the people I would see walking down the street, it was keeping me at a distance from her when we were alone together. It was an unrealized blockade impeding my ability to be as close to her as I want to be. There is no such impediment now, and I am engulfing myself inside her.

The feel of my cheeks nuzzled in between hers makes this moment seem so...sweet. It's nice. I don't know how else to describe it. It's just kind of...pure. That's how I feel. That's what I think.

I also feel like one good rimming deserves another.

So, moving my head in tiny circles around her ass, just like she did to me a couple of days ago, I get off on the whining noises she makes, and I work two fingers inside her pussy to help everybody along. With my other hand I begin fisting my cock. I'm trying to go slowly so that I don't fucking come right here all over the Mandarin's nice carpet. I already burned down one of their condos, I don't want to fuck up one of their suites too. New-look Tyler is considerate like that. But as slowly as I'm *trying* to go, she's making it tough because of the way she's rotating her ass and hips around.

And suddenly, I don't want to be behind her. I mean, I love the view from here and I *love* the way she tastes, but I want to see her. I want to look at her face and have her look at mine. Yeah. I want her to look at me. I want her to see me.

So I pull away, flop down on my back on the bed beside her, and summon to her with my index finger to come over. She does, smiling as she mounts me. She takes my two fingers that were just inside her and puts them in her mouth. And I remember the first time I saw her do that. I told her, "You're going to fucking kill me." But she didn't. She didn't. It was exactly the opposite. She fucking saved me. And so now, with her astride me, I sit up, take her face in my hands, look her square in the eyes, and tell her, "I fucking love you."

She closes her own eyes with a shy smile and whispers, "I fucking love you."

And as she wraps her legs completely around the back of me, locking her ankles into place and grinding back and forth while I thrust up and into her, I keep looking into her eyes and feel only one thing... gratitude.

Well, that and the slightly numbing pain that rolls up and down my side as her body contracts against mine in orgasm and my muscles tense and spasm as, at the same time, I erupt inside her, come pouring out of me, commingling with her release quicker than if I was a goddamn thirteen-year-old. Ecstasy and agony competing for dominance with the threat of happiness looming in the background.

And once again, I find myself... here. Just here. Present, and quiet, and still. And I think that I could get used to this feeling. And I am so, so, so grateful.

As my dick pulses and clenches inside her, expelling the last bits of my orgasm, I feel emotion that I can't manage welling up inside. "Thank you," I sigh out.

"You're welcome," she says on a tiny smile, her body still quivering and gyrating as she slows down from our shared explosion. "Thank *you*."

"No," I say, stilling her with my hands on her face again. She looks at me quizzically. "I'm not just saying it. What I mean is—"

She takes my face in her hands now, presses her forehead against mine and, so quietly I can barely hear, she whispers, "I know."

She smiles. I smile. And then she says, "Sorry that was so quick."

"I was just gonna say the same thing," I tell her. "But you..."

She grins a shy little smile. And that gets my engine revving one more time.

"You wanna go again?" I ask her.

"Are you serious?" she says with wide-eyed glee.

"Unkillable python is still hungry."

"It is? Oh, no! And me without my snake charmer's flute."

"Baby, you *are* a fucking snake charmer's flute," I tell her.

And bless her heart, she has the decency to laugh at my stupid, cheesy joke as she commences grinding her sweet, sweet melody into my cock.

And as she swerves against me, playing her seductive song, the unkillable python resurrects itself to prove once more that its reputation is well-deserved.

CHAPTER ELEVEN

There's no one at the door to the suite when I open it. The doorbell rang, but when I got there, the hallway was empty. Just a bottle of wine, already open, with two glasses filled, and some roses next to it sitting on a room service cart. Not even a card or anything. I assume it's from the hotel. Hotels do that kind of shit when you spend a fuck-ton of money out of the blue.

I guess the good news is that if they're sending us fancy amenities, they haven't yet put together that I'm the same dude who torched one of their penthouse residences. I have a hard time imagining that they'd be super-quick to gift me if they realized I was the brother responsible for burning up a three-million-dollar apartment. Or maybe the wine is, like, poisoned or something and it's their way of getting back at me.

That'd be some fucked up, passive-aggressive bullshit. And while that's a crazy thought and, I know, totally not the case, now I'm paranoid and decide that's it better to be safe than sorry and push the cart into the corner of the living room. I'm starting to think that all the shit that went down with Carlos and Logan has me a little more shook than I've allowed myself to admit. I walk over to the windows and look out.

Staring down at all the people scurrying around on the street below as the sun starts to set feels different than it did from my apartment just a short time ago. Watching them then filled me with...contempt maybe? I held everyone in the world accountable for the shitty way that I felt. Because that's what victims do. They also don't usually see themselves as victims. That's the bitch. The anger masks the hurt.

Yeah, I was a real fucking delight.

Stop it, dude. That's just a different version of the same song.

Fair enough, brain voice. Fair enough.

But watching everyone now fills me with...I dunno. Curiosity, I suppose? I wonder what they're all up to. I wonder what they're doing. I wonder why. It's crazy, I've been all over the earth twice and I'm not really sure I've actually seen it. Which is corny as hell, but it's how it strikes me now. I've been taught things about people and about life, but I don't know if I learned anything about either until very, very recently.

I look up and see Maddie's reflection appear in the darkening window. She's silhouetted by the light from the entrance to the bathroom where she just took a shower. She's wearing one of the big, puffy Mandarin Oriental robes with the little Asian fan on the left breast, her long, red hair flowing down over the shawl collar. The Radiohead song *Creep* begins playing in bits and pieces in my head.

You're just like an angel. I'm a weirdo. What the hell am I doing here? I don't belong here.

Except that for the first time...I feel like maybe I do.

Shit. We all do.

I don't turn around. She wraps her arms around me and rests her head against my shoulder. "You're dressed."

I nod. "Yeah."

"You don't wanna take a shower?"

"Nah, I like smelling like you."

She strokes my arm with her fingertips. "Does it bother you that I took a shower?"

"Why would it bother me?"

She shrugs her shoulders into me. "I dunno. You don't think I'm trying to wash the smell off or anything, do you?"

I screw my expression up. That thought honestly would never have occurred to me in a million years. "No. I think you're, like, a clean, classy woman and I'm a filthy, lazy dude."

"OK. Good," she says and hugs me tighter. "Whatcha thinking about?" she asks.

I breathe in deeply and let it out through my nose. "I dunno. Just...us."

"'Us,' you and me? Or the royal 'us?'"

"Both, I suppose."

We're quiet for a moment as we watch the world continue to turn with the sound of vaguely Asian-sounding, sexy spa music playing in the background. That's what they pipe all through the Mandarin. It sounds like what would happen if someone took a Japanese shamisen and, I dunno, tried to fuck it. But I don't mind it right now. It's nice.

"What about all of us?" she asks.

"Nothing, really. No judgment. Just that we're here, I suppose. And how fuckin' weird that all is."

"Yeah," she says, hugging me tighter still. "It's fucked up all right."

I put my hand on her wrists where she's gripping me and realize that she's still wearing the watch. I hadn't really paid attention, but now it hits me that I don't think she's taken it off since we got back from Mexico.

"Did it start running again?" I ask.

"What?"

"Nadir's watch. Is it keeping time again?"

She pulls her arm free from around me and looks. "Nope," she says. "Still stopped." She shows it to me. "Does it need a new battery?"

I shake my head. "No battery. It's automatic. It stays charged up or whatever by just being worn. The movement of your wrist is what keeps it running."

"What happens when you take it off?"

"It builds up reserves and goes for a while until it runs out of juice. I dunno. I ain't no kinda horologist, it just got explained to me one time. But if it's not working, something inside musta gotten fucked up."

"Well, there was all kinds of gunfire and explosions and slamming into walls and the ground and stuff."

I take a moment to ponder and say, "Yeah, none of that would account for it."

She laughs and starts to elbow me in the side, but then catches herself and stops. I wonder how goddamn long it's gonna take for the tenderness in my ribs to go away. It's been almost four days already. Christ, I must be getting old.

"You wanna try to get it fixed?" she asks.

"Sure," I say. "We could. You know a place?"

She nods at the huge Gucci sign just across the street that sits on the corner of a bunch of fancy stores that are connected to the Mandarin by a walkway. "There's a watch place in there, isn't there?"

"Where?" I ask. "Over in the mall?" She laughs. "What? What's funny?"

"You called it 'the mall,'" she says.

It's this crazy shopping monstrosity that got built while I was away. Vegas changed a fuckton in the years I was gone. It had started its family-friendly conversion before I left, but by the time I came back, I almost didn't recognize it. Somewhere over the years, retail stores figured out that people with money come to Vegas, and those people gamble and get drunk and are stupid with their money, and that the opportunity was there to grab a piece of that action.

'What happens in Vegas, stays in Vegas' is basically in reference to your fuckin' paycheck. That's the part they leave out of the slogan.

"Yeah?" I say, in reference to her mocking tone about me calling it 'a mall.' "Why? What do you call it?"

"Boutiques? Shops? I dunno. Everything in there is super high-end. I just thought it was cute that you called it a mall."

"Whatever. It's got stores and shit, and people wander around in there like brain-dead zombies out of *Dawn of the Dead*. It's a fuckin' mall."

Semantics.

"Fair enough," she says.

"I can maybe get behind calling it 'the Asshole Mall.'"

She smiles and steps in front to face me, puts both hands on my cheeks. "Do you want to swing into the Asshole Mall and see if there's a place that can fix your watch?"

"Nadir's watch."

"Nadir's watch?"

She grins up at me with this impish expression and

for a flash of a moment I'm transported back to Halloween night. Before she and I hooked up. Like, maybe an hour before when I was at the station house with Evan and there was a little kid dressed up like Charlie Chaplin from *The Tramp*. I thought about how cute he was and that I just wanted to eat his fucking head. That's how I feel about Maddie right now. She is equal parts sexy, and kind, and adorable, and I get that sense that no matter how much of her I take into my life, however greedy I get, it will never be enough. And I realize...

She's all I need. I don't need another fucking thing. Me and her and I'm good. And on the heels of that, an idea starts percolating.

"Yeah," I say. "Yeah, let's fix Nadir's watch."

Watch girl at the watch place in the Asshole Mall seemed to know what she was doing. She was Chinese and made a joke about Chinese women being the best at watch repair because of their attention to detail and their little fingers. Funny thing is she's totally not wrong. But she has to make that joke, 'cause I sure as fuck ain't gonna be the one to make it.

Maddie rightly noted that the reason I trusted her is not because I thought she was necessarily capable, but because I thought she was funny. Maddie's right. That is why. But it's not as random as one might think. It's because funny people – like really, genuinely *funny* people – in my experience, get that life itself is absurd. That's *why* they joke about it. Because this whole fucking dance we all do with each other is so fabricated and ludicrous that to not make fun of it feels like the thing that is actually the most laughable.

And shit, watch girl made a joke in a *second language*. Yo, if you've got the ability to be sarcastic in a language that's not even your native tongue? Then you is one smart motherfucker and I will trust you to perform a goddamn appendectomy on me if you want. (I mean, presuming you're also a doctor and shit.)

Maddie and I are now sitting in a coffee shop on the lower level of the Asshole Mall, drinking a couple of five-dollar coffees like the assholes we are. They're fucking tasty though, I will admit. Mine's pumpkin spice or some shit.

"Hey," I start. "I had this idea."

"Yeah?"

"Yeah. Um, after we get the watch back next week or whatever, there's something I'd like to do. But only if it's OK with you, and if It is, I'd love it if you'd do it with me."

"Yeah?" she says. "What is it?"

"I know I gave it to you to have for Mexico, but now that you're here and you're safe, I'd like to... give it back."

She tilts her head slightly. "Give it back to...?"

"Nadir. Or Nadir's family. I'd like to make a trip and find Nadir's family and give it to them. I mean, I just... They should have it."

I wasn't expecting tears to start welling up in her eyes at this, but they do. She nods. "Yeah. Yeah. That sounds like a great idea."

"Yeah? You think?"

She nods tightly now, pressing her lips together, and sniffing back a tear or two. "Yeah. I think."

"Cool. And also—"

117

"Oh, Christ, there's more? I don't wanna cry in the middle of the Asshole Mall."

Holy shit. I love her so, so, so much.

"I just..." I go on, risking her making a spectacle of herself. "Did I tell you what Nadir wanted to do with his money when we got it?" She shakes her head. "Well, like, everything. Like build irrigation systems in his town, and fund infrastructure projects, and build schools for girls and shit."

Her eyes light up at that last one. "Really?"

"Yeah, really. And so... I mean I've got all this fuckin' money and at least half of it is his whether he's here or not, and I don't even want all this fuckin' money, so while we're over there... You see where I'm going with this?"

I'm assuming the kiss she gives me as she jumps up and almost knocks over the table with our asshole coffees means that she does know where I'm going with it.

"What was that for?" I ask when she finally pulls away.

She doesn't answer directly. She just takes her index finger and pokes me on the chest over my heart and says, "This. Fuckin' this."

I'm fighting every urge inside myself to deflect or make a joke right now, or somehow change the subject. Because there are lots of ways to show a person that you love them. And one of those ways is by sitting in your discomfort with a situation and putting your agenda aside to allow the person you love to have their own feelings. (Dr. Eldridge taught me that. Which reminds me, I have to call Dr. Eldridge and tell her I'm cured. She's gonna be stoked.)

And shit, as long as this is the kind of conversation we're having...

"So," I say. "I should also tell you something else."

She looks like she's about to make a wisecrack herself, but she must sense that I'm being pretty serious because she just lowers her mint-infused whatever-the-fuck from her lips, sets it down on the table between us, leans in, and says, "K. What's up?"

New-look Tyler, new-look Tyler, new-look Tyler.

"Uh, the reason that I don't live at The Mandarin anymore..." Fuck. I really don't want to do this, but I have to.

"Yeah?" She encourages me to continue.

I take a massive breath. "Is because... you know the night you split? Halloween?"

She nods. "Yeah. Rings a bell." I appreciate so much that she's trying to make this easy for me.

"Yeah, right, well... So after we... And you... And then you left... Are you following me?"

She nods and leans over to take my hands in hers, "More or less. Helps that I was there."

"Right, right," I say. "So after you split... I might've gone a little... um. Insane."

She nods, blinking twice as she does. "K. What does that mean? Exactly?"

"Um. When we pulled up to the valet earlier, did you happen to look up?"

"Up? Uh, no. We were pretty much racing to get to Brown Chicken Brown Cow."

"Heh, right. Bow-chica-bow-wow. Right. Um, well, if you had looked up, you might've seen a bunch of slabs of wood boarding up the place where the windows of my apartment used to be." I give a toothy smile. Nervous habit.

She sort of sucks at her teeth. "Mm-hm. Why?" she

asks, cautiously.

"Because of the fire."

"Uh-huh. Which fire?"

"The one I started after you left."

She lifts her hand to her forehead and draws it all the way down her face until it drops from her chin. I take a sip of my coffee, although I'm not sure I need the caffeine just at present.

"Say again?" she says.

"Honestly, I'm not a hundred percent sure I can walk you through it. The whole thing is a little hazy. But I just wanted you to know that that's what happened after you left. I went a little crazy and I may have started a fire in my place. Truthfully, I've kind of lost time a bit. So. Yeah."

There's a long moment where she says nothing. Long enough for me to take two sips of caffeine that I probably don't need. Finally, she says...

"And that's why you're at Evan's."

"That's why I'm at Evan's."

"Because you burned down your apartment."

"That is what happened, it seems."

She now takes up her drink and continues nodding a tiny bit as she takes a sip. Then she places it back down on the table, wipes her mouth with her hand, and says, "Well, shit. That was the same night I voluntarily wandered into a car with a drug dealer and assumed I was gonna be hacked to bits or sold into sex slavery, so I guess who the fuck am I to judge?"

I have to bite my bottom lip to the point that it's almost bleeding to keep from smiling. But then she smiles, which gives me permission, and then we're both laughing. We probably look like a couple of assholes, but if so, we're in the perfect place. After a moment, the laughter dies down and she says, "Can I ask you something?"

"Sure," I say, still smiling.

"Have you ever been to Scotty's grave?" And now, suddenly, I'm not smiling. "Like, since you've been back, or...?"

Rather than answer directly, I say, "What made you think to ask that?"

She shrugs an 'I dunno' shrug. Except that she does know. We both do.

"No," I say, candidly, trying not to make any excuses. "No. I haven't."

"I haven't been for a while either." She looks ashamed.

"Maybe that's something we should do, then."

"Yeah. Yeah. Maybe it is."

We just stare at each other for a tick until the moment is broken by the sound of a text message pinging my phone. I pick it up off the table and look at the screen. The message says it's from one of those weird short code numbers that telemarketers will sometimes use. This one is 87-3323.

The message reads, "Plans for New Year's?"

I know this is just some bullshit solicitation text. I get them all the time, even though I've put myself on the damn Do Not Call registry like twice. The thing is, they're just sending out this shit scattershot, and if you call or text back, *now* they've got your actual phone number locked. So as tempting as it is to "text 1 to opt out," or whatever, as soon as you do, they'll have your digits and then you're fucked.

And, again, even though I know that's what this is, something about getting the text makes me uneasy. The same way seeing my dad the day after tomorrow is making me uneasy. I'm chalking it all up to the fact that Maddie and I have just been through a fucking lot and on top of that some major changes are coming our way, but the reminder that the new year is right around the corner and that I'm cautiously hopeful that this new year will bring the peace that Evan is always wishing for me is making me feel just a little unsettled. Which is, I suppose, ironic.

"Who is it?" Maddie asks.

I swipe to delete the text and say, "Nobody. Bullshit solicitor. You ready to go, asshole?"

"Yeah, asshole. Let's get the fuck out of here."

We both stand, throw our half-finished drinks in the trash, and take each other's hands. She gives me a kiss on the lips, then rubs her fingers once again across my naked face. "So you just spent almost eleven thousand dollars to spend four hours in a building that you used to own an apartment in before you burned it down."

I blow my lips out. "That does seem to be the case."

She runs her fingers through my hair. "Yeah. You're gonna need to build at least two or three girls' schools, my friend."

And with that, we saunter our way up the escalator and out the door.

Just two assholes making their way in the world.

CHAPTER TWELVE

MADDIE

December 29th
Two Days Until New Year's Eve

"You OK?" Tyler asks as we drive north on I-15 towards the cemetery. He reaches for my hand and gives it a squeeze.

"Yeah," I say, forcing a smile. "I'm cool." I'm not cool. In fact, I might be falling apart. Right here. In this car. On this freeway. Going to...

I look at Tyler, fake smile still in place.

He smiles back, except I'm pretty sure his is real, then he takes his attention back to the drive. There's a ton of traffic so he changes lanes.

I take his distraction as a time to pull myself together and *reflect*. Not on Scotty. Not really. More about how long it's been since I've visited his grave. How guilty that makes me feel. Like I'm the worst sister in the world.

Four years. I count the anniversaries. Yeah, four. The last time I was here I was selling make-up online. That was the year I got the idea for the pet bakery, so I was trying to figure out how I could talk my parents into lending me money. I'd blown through all my savings and maxed out seven credit cards on other stupid ideas.

That was two years after they left for France and one year after I totaled their car. Well, my car, I guess. They signed it over to me when they moved away.

I never told them about that. Just started taking the bus. I was waitressing at the Hard Rock and living in a pay-by-the-week motel just off the strip so I could be close to my job. It took me three years to save up money and rebuild my credit enough to buy the little Honda I had been driving last Halloween.

Which I no longer have because I left it in the middle of the street and went home with Tyler.

God, what was I thinking? Not about Tyler. He's pretty much the best thing to happen to me in... maybe ever. But leaving my car like that was so irresponsible. So reckless. And crazy.

And all those words pretty much sum up the last seven years perfectly.

"How long?" Tyler asks, pulling me out of my self-reflection.

"Four years," I say. "Funny. I was just thinking about it."

"What were you doing four years ago?" Tyler looks over at me, but then quickly takes his attention to the road when the car in front of us slams on their brakes. "Fuck," he says, changing lanes again.

"Four years ago..." Four years ago I was declaring bankruptcy. I was dead-ass broke. I was... unrecognizable. "I was selling make-up online."

"Really? How was that?"

Wow. There's still so much we don't yet know about each other. Which kind of makes me excited, actually. Because it means there's a lot to learn.

"Pretty good," I say, nodding my head.

"Why'd you stop?"

"Oh." I wave my hand in the air. "They went out of business. Left me with a shitload of stock too. Which I did sell on Ebay eventually."

I just got rid of the last of that stock about six months ago. Which is ironic, because the very day I made that final sale—if you can call losing a hundred percent of the price I paid for it a "sale"—I had a drink with Annie. We bumped into each other at the post office and then drove over to a little bar to catch up since I was avoiding my wedding planner job after the Carlos shit started going sideways. And I told her all about my big online makeup venture and how it was over now, and I was a wedding planner but had another new idea, and we toasted to new beginnings.

That's when she mentioned she needed a roommate.

Weird. How two completely unrelated things can become related.

I sure did get a new beginning, and I'm not complaining about how it all turned out, but... Jesus. So much has happened in that short period of time.

Tyler says, "If I'd had been here I'd have bought all the makeup."

"Really? And done what with it?"

"Dunno. But you'd be driving a pink Caddie right now."

God, I love him. "Thanks for this."

"For what?"

"Coming with me to the grave."

"You're coming with *me*." Then he squeezes my hand again. "But yeah. It's hard."

I nod, refusing to cry. "Yeah," I say. "It's hard."

"Does it get any easier?" he asks.

"No," I say. And now it's my turn to squeeze *his* hand. "At least it hasn't yet. But I'm glad you're here."

He sighs through his nose. Nods. Goes silent as he probably runs the past several years through his mind too.

In a way, life is like those dumb choose-your-own-adventure books we found in the closet. Sell makeup online, turn to page 34. Total your car, turn back to page 16. Fail at the make-up business, go back to start. Meet an old friend at the post office, skip to page 200. Get caught up in a drug lord's crazy, go back to start. Get a job stripping at Pete's, go to page 90. Fall in love with your childhood crush…

Then what?

That's like the happily ever after, right? Achieving your goals isn't the end, it's supposed to be a beginning. Isn't it?

So back to the start, I guess. "Book two. Page one."

"What?" Tyler says. He looks over at me, smiling. Either his past four years have been better than mine—which I doubt—or he's putting on a brave front for my sake. Just like the one I'm putting on for him.

"You know. Those choose-your-own-adventure books. We met, we did…all this, and now what? We're at the end of the book. Commander Morgan has swept the Space Goddess off her feet and now what?"

He chuckles. Just a little one, but I'm pretty sure it's real. "Book two. Page one."

"Yeah," I say.

We squeeze each other's hands as he gets off the freeway. Less than a minute later I can see the cemetery off to the right and I begin to sweat, even though it's cool out today.

"The last time I came here I was drunk. I said a lot of mean things to him. Like really shitty things."

I didn't mean to admit that. But fuck it. If I can't tell Tyler about these things, then who can I tell? Plumeria Brown? No, thank you.

"I was drunk for the funeral too. I barely remember it. I know it was special. I know there was a color guard and cannons or whatever it is they fire to memorialize firefighters killed in the line of duty. I know there were a lot of men in uniform. And lots of crying. I know I got up halfway through the burial and left. Just walked away. My dad came looking for me in the car. I was almost to the freeway and... I don't know where I was going. Like was I just gonna stumble onto the freeway? Where was I going?"

I pause to look at Tyler. As if he has the answer to this question. But it's ridiculous because he wasn't even there. And I know that's what he's thinking about. How he wasn't there. And now we're probably both thinking about all the things between then and now. All the failures. All the mistakes. All the sadness. All the—

"I'm so, so, so sorry I wasn't there, Maddie."

"Me too," I whisper, my eyes already searching for the grave as we turn into the cemetery entrance. I point to the road that goes off to the left and he turns. "It would've been better if we'd had each other." He nods.

Silence as I guide him the rest of the way to the grave by pointing my finger until we reach Scotty's row and he stops the car.

Turns it off.

Silence.

Stillness.

"We're here," I say.

"Yeah, we are," he replies.

We get out of the car at the same time. Meet at the entrance to the row and find each other's hands. Squeezing tight, together.

I have a sudden stab of fear now that we're here. I want to get back in the car. I want to drive home. I want to go back to bed, bury my face in the pillows, and cry and never stop.

I want to go back to the start.

Tyler says, "Visit your best friend's grave, turn to page 99."

This makes me keep walking. "That's quite a jump. Sure it's not page 23?"

"Nah," Tyler says, focused on the grave markers and headstones. He already knows Scotty's headstone is light grey and stands about waist tall because I told him before we left. So he passes by all the small, ground-level markers. "This is a monumental leap forward in pages for Commander Morgan."

Fuck it. I decide to play along. It's kinda fun. And better than dwelling on all the mistakes and failures. "Admit your brother didn't die on purpose, turn to page 199."

"Let go of the guilt of not being there, turn to page 256," Tyler whispers.

"Take responsibility for your actions, turn to page 301."

I start to cry. We stop walking and he just holds me, whispering in my ear, "You're OK, you're OK, you're

OK," over and over again until I start nodding my head against his chest, trying to talk myself into believing it.

"I miss him," I sob. "I just really miss him."

Tyler drags a stray piece of hair away from my cheek and tucks it behind my ear. Then he kisses my head and says, "Me too. But..." I can feel him swallow hard. Feel him take a deep, deep breath. Feel him rally, for my sake, or his sake, or someone's sake. And he says, "Come on."

I back away, nodding. Sniffling. Wiping my wet cheeks. And then I turn, find his grave with my eyes just a few yards away, and pull myself together as I approach.

His name and date of last call is like a dark scar carved into the granite. Above that is a quote. *For those I love, I shall sacrifice.*

A hot flash of anger rides up my spine and makes the hair on the back of my neck stand on end. I go stiff. Bristling at my brother's choices.

Tyler's hand on my shoulder cools me off.

I take a deep breath, then drop to my knees and press my fingers into the creed. Tracing each letter. Letting go of my anger. Accepting that this was his love. He loved fighting fires. And he did make the ultimate sacrifice. But that was his choice. Maybe it was a bad one—for sure it was a bad one. But I've made so many bad choices, who am I to judge?

But then I remember he saved someone. That guy— I forget his name. Jim something, I think. He saved Jim. Sacrificed himself. And then I recall Brandon... Raven's Brandon. He had a sticker on the back of his helmet that night he pulled Jeff out of the fire at Pete's. It read, *So that brothers and others may live.*

"He was a hero," I say. More to Tyler, but it's Scotty I'm talking to. "You *are* my hero."

And then I cry some more.

And the words pour out like water. "Scotty," I say to him, still tracing the letter of his headstone quote. "God. I've seen a lot of fire over the past month. People have died in it. Some good, some bad. I don't think I've ever seen so much fire."

I look over my shoulder to find Tyler has stepped back. He's leaning up against a tree, arms across his chest. Our eyes meet and he smiles with only his lips and then nods for me to keep going. So I do.

"I know I haven't been here in a long time but I just want you to know, it's got nothing to do with you, OK? It's me. Because... because I wanted you to be proud of me and I couldn't come back here until I was proud of myself. Until I was brave again. Until I was strong again. I never wanted you to see me the way you saw me last. Drunk at the funeral, then drunk again on the anniversary. I wanted to make you proud. I wanted to show you that I was OK. And it just took me a while. I'm sorry about that. But I'm doing better, I think."

I drag the back of my hand across my nose, wiping away the running snot. "And guess what?" I smile, then find myself laughing. "Guess who's here with me?"

I look over my shoulder to see Tyler. He looks... scared.

"It's Tyler. He came home. He's still alive. He's been through hell and back, but he's still here. And... and I don't really know how to tell you this, but we're together now." I pause. I'm not sure why. Maybe I'm waiting for a reaction. "And it's good. It's good," I say. "It's really good. So I hope that makes you happy. That he's back. That I've got him back. I just want you know that I'm safe, and I'm actually happy. For the first time since... since I last saw you. I think I'm going to be OK."

I have books of things to say to him. I want to tell him about Carlos and the drone. About how we—or someone—blew up the fueling station and took down the compound. About how Tyler has my back now. How I feel safe with him. Protected and cherished. How he makes me laugh with his quirky weirdness. How I think we're made for each other. And how he might be the one. Might be? No. He *is* the one.

But I don't say any of that. I just trace his name and his last call date. I whisper his motto. And then I put my arms around his headstone and give him a hug. Because I think he needs a hug.

"I miss you," I say, pretending he's here. That he's hugging me back. That he never left.

Because that's all I *can* do.

CHAPTER THIRTEEN

TYLER

Watching her rips me up inside. I had no idea it would be like this for her. I'm starting to realize that there's actually a whole, whole lot I don't know about Maddie anymore. Lots of details to fill in. Shit, lots of details about me to fill in for her. But that's OK, because that image I had in Mexico of me marrying her and being with her – assuming I didn't die, which I didn't – still looms large for me.

If I'm being truthful, there was a moment where I wondered if I'd wake up and not feel that way anymore. If it was just the desperation of the circumstance we were in that was causing those thoughts to manifest. I mean, that shit happens. Circumstances change and feelings change with them. I'm not naïve. Hell, could happen for her too. We could leave here today, she could remember all the ways I totally hung her out to dry, and she could feel completely differently about me than she did the day before.

Except I doubt it. Because what I feel for her right now is a love that's not born out of desire, or want, or even need. Yeah, sure, there's passion. Bet your ass there's fucking passion. I want her all the time, but that's not what

I feel now. What I feel now is greater than that. Elevated. More.

What I want now is just to be near her. To help her when she wants, to let her be when that's what she needs, and to learn to be just a little less stupid. (But only a little, because my idiocy is part of my charm. Not everybody says so, but I believe it's true.)

And I've made it this far in life on my wits, such as they are, and my intuition, which isn't terrible. And my gut tells me that she's here to stay. And I am one hundred percent here to stay with her as long as she'll have me.

She lets go of her bear hug on Scotty's headstone and crosses over to where I'm standing. Her cheeks are streaked with her tears and it makes her look like a kid somehow. I see all of her at once. Who she was, who she is, who she will become. And while I'm tempted to wipe her tears away, I don't. Because they're hers. And she should be able to hold them as long as she needs. I don't even crack a joke to try to make her feel better or anything. Because sometimes what a person needs most is understanding. Not healing.

I'm learning, Pete. I'm learning.

She stands in front of me, not saying anything, and finally I ask, "You cool if I—?" I gesture over to Scotty's grave.

She nods. "Yeah. I kinda just wanna sit here for a minute anyway."

"Copy," I say, and then feel out if she wants me all up on her or if she wants to be left alone for a sec. She steps up and puts her arms around me, so I just wrap her up until she lets go. And then we hold hands for as long as possible until our fingertips slip away from each other and I move to the headstone.

It feels massive as I approach. It's not. Not really. It's just a normal-sized memorial. But it gets bigger and bigger with each step I take. And each step I take feels like five normal steps. I don't even know if that makes sense, but it's certainly how it feels.

When I land at the plot, I walk all around it. I'm not sure why, but I wander behind the marble slab, examining it from all angles. I'm just making sure it's all OK. Like, suddenly I don't completely trust the groundskeepers or whoever to keep it all pristine.

But it is. It's fine. It's beautiful, in fact. Which I'm glad about. I didn't expect it to be otherwise, but still. It's nice.

And now I don't know what to do. I mean, I don't know if I should pray or... Praying seems disingenuous. Because it's just not me. And because even though I've dreamed of Heaven and possibly even died and been to Heaven, I'm still not so sure I believe in all that shit. So praying feels like it's out.

I could just, like, *be* here. Just stand here and commune with the air and the grass and the trees and just absorb the world as it continues to turn. And, in doing that, maybe that honors Scotty's memory. A certain amount of deferential stillness on my part would certainly be dignified. But that's also not really me. I suppose it could be, but it feels out of place somehow right now.

I guess, if I examine what I want, I feel like I want to say something. Like, actually talk to Scotty like he's still here. Even though that seems cliché and maybe even a little hokey. Because I don't know if Scotty would be able to hear me anyway. Is the consciousness that was Scotty Clayton still somewhere in this vast expanse of cosmic dust? Does it matter? Is it even Scotty that I'm here for? Or is it me? Is it Maddie?

Fuck it. Who gives a shit?

"Hey, dude," I say. "Sorry it took me so long to swing by, but... as you already know, I'm a terrible person."

I don't say any of this loud enough for Maddie to hear. For a lot of reasons, but not least of all because this ain't a performance. This is just for me and Scotty. Or maybe just for me.

"Um, so... I guess I should fill you in on everything since there's no one else who's been able to... Fuck." I trail off because, well, because I feel shitty. Then I start back up because, well, because I have to.

"I guess the first thing is that I'm back. Back in Vegas. As you can tell, because, y'know, I'm here." This is going very well. Christ.

I hang my head. And then I decide to just let it out.

"Look, man, if you're somewhere that you can hear me or, shit, even if you're not, here's the thing I wanna say. For a while now, I've been carrying this fuckin' belief around with me that what happened to you was my fault. Right? Like because I fucked with you and joked around about stuff that it somehow drove you to make the decisions you made. And that if I hadn't been the way I was — with you, I mean — that you'd be alive now. And here's what I wanna say about that."

I crack my neck side to side, then look over my shoulder and see Maddie, sitting under the tree with her eyes closed. I nod a tiny bit and then look back at the grave and resume.

"What I wanna say is... who the fuck do I think I am? Y'know? Like, how the fuck do I think that I'm *so* powerful and important that you made your life decisions based on *me* and whatever the fuck I said? That's messed up, right? You don't have to answer. Rhetorical. But, yeah, it's fucked up. It's arrogant and narcissistic and yet at the same time happens to be chickenshit. Which, I mean, that's no small achievement, so I guess I can at least be proud of what a trifecta of bullshit I managed to pull off for so long."

I'm kind of cooking now, so I keep going. I might be getting a little louder than I want to, but I don't care.

"Because all I really did was use what happened to you as an excuse to wallow in my own sad, lost, failed travesty of a life. And know why that's fucked up? Of course you do, but I'll say it anyway. It's because it fucking diminishes you twice. First, it makes it seem like you weren't your own person, and second, it then uses you to allow me to be as worthless a person as I could manage to be. And for that... Fuck. Sorry doesn't cut it, but it's really all I got. So. Sorry."

I blow a breath out through my lips.

"And the bitch of it is that I totally know you'd forgive me. Because you were always the bigger man. The better man. And... Shit. Something I never told you... I always looked up to you. I did. Because in all the ways that matter, you were the kind of person I wanted to be. You and Evan. I dunno why the two of you ever decided to keep me around. But you did. And I will be forever grateful for that. Because any good in me, anything that I learned about how to be a good person or a good friend... anything after Mom died, at least... I owe to you two assholes. I don't think I ever said that. But I'm not sure I knew it before. So. I'm sorry. But, yeah, now you know."

It feels like my brain itches. But I think maybe what I'm doing right now is actually scratching it. So once again, I keep going.

"And, I suppose, this is particularly important for you to hear because... I don't know if Maddie mentioned it, but... We're... I'm... She and I... You get where I'm going with this, right? We're together now. Like, a couple and shit. And... and this is the important part, OK? So stay with me. I love her. I love her. Like, a lot. Like, I couldn't see the shit coming, but here it is, and I love her. And I really, *really* hope you're good with that. Because, like... and I hesitate to use this phrasing for reasons that will become apparent quickly, but... she gave me my life back, man."

I glance over my shoulder again. She still has her eyes closed. I again turn my head toward the grave.

"She gave me my life back, dude." This time, I say it barely above a whisper. "She saved me when I thought I was past the point of saving." Pete's words coming through my mouth.

"And I hope you're OK with it. Which of course you are, because you're awesome and you just want the best for people. Fucking dick." I shake my head and smile.

"I suppose there's a shit-ton more to say, but... hey, man, I can't make up for the past, which you well know. And I can't foretell the future, which you also well know. But I can do my best to be here, in the breathing present, and make this world, as I know it now, the best it can possibly be. Or at least I can try that with my little corner of it, right? Oh! And I totally forgot to say... I'm super fucking rich now. Yeah. I am. So when I say that I can make the world a better place and shit, I actually *can*. So, I'm gonna do that, I think. And I'm gonna do it with Maddie. We're gonna do it together. We're gonna try to live in your image, bro. And I hope that you're OK with that too."

Now that I'm at the end of my fucked-up little graveside homily, I start feeling self-conscious about everything I just said out loud. I find myself shuffling my feet and kind of looking around, and then I look back at the headstone and say, "Dude? If you actually were able to hear any of this... can you give me some kind of sign? Or whatever?"

I hold my breath. Not intentionally. It's just what happens. I don't know what I'm expecting. Like, a dove or some shit to land on the grave marker. Or a gentle breeze to suddenly blow through. Or, hell, Scotty's voice to come from out of nowhere and go, "Bro, don't sweat it. We're cool."

But none of that happens. Nothing happens. No dove, no cool breeze, no disembodied voice from the heavens. Just the sound of traffic in the distance and of maybe a leaf-blower somewhere nearby. The grounds crew tending to everyone's lost friends, family, and lovers.

And then, after a few long moments, I let out the breath I've been holding in and say, "Yeah. OK." And then I turn and head back to where Maddie sits.

"Hey," I say as quietly as I can when I approach. Her eyes flutter open.

"Hey."

"You wanna stay here anymore, or...?"

She looks up at me and shakes her head. "No. I'm good."

"Are you?"

"I dunno."

I sigh and nod.

"But," she goes on, "I think maybe I will be."

I nod some more. "Yeah."

She reaches her hand up to me. I take it and help pull her to her feet. When she lands, she falls forward into my arms and leans up to give me a kiss. She strokes her hand down the side of my still freshly naked cheek and says, "Thank you."

"Shit," I say, my brow furrowed. "For what?"

"For being here. Even though it's hard."

"Hell. This isn't hard—" I start, with the intention of enumerating for her all the things we've gotten up to lately that have been *much* harder. But she cuts me off.

"Yeah, it is."

I don't challenge her. I just nod once again and give her another kiss.

"It's a privilege," I say. "I mean, that's what commitment is."

"What?"

"Showing up. Even when shit ain't easy. Especially when shit ain't easy."

She closes her eyes and presses her forehead against my chest. I can feel her nodding into me as I stroke her hair. And then, without looking up at me, her muffled voice mumbles out.

"I love you."

With her face as close to my chest as it is, I wonder if she can hear my heart break.

"I love you too," I manage to croak.

She looks up at me and says, "You ready?" I nod slowly and give her one more kiss on the head.

She takes my hand in hers, and we begin walking to the car.

And as we walk, it's probably just in my mind, but I swear I can feel a tiny breeze at our backs, pushing us along.

CHAPTER FOURTEEN

MADDIE

December 30th
One Day Until New Year's Eve

"OK, great, thank you very much," I say before hanging up the phone.

I was just talking with the Afghan Foreign Ministry and am a little surprised to discover that getting visas for me and Tyler basically just requires filling out an application. I thought for sure that Tyler would have to pull some strings with someone at, like, The State Department or something, but apparently not. In fact, they actually seemed more shocked that I was so eager to come for a visit.

Two months ago, I was working in a strip club, dreaming about how to get my real estate drone business off the ground and today I'm working on getting travel visas for me and Tyler Morgan to go to Afghanistan and build schools for girls.

This year is not ending up at all the way I would have imagined.

I'm finding myself thinking about my life more than I ever have. More accurately, thinking about my future.

Which is new for me because I don't feel like I really believed before that I had much of a future, so I never spent much time considering it. It was always just about putting one foot in front of the other. And now, I'm making plans to, like, try and help change the world. Wow.

I remember once there was a big Powerball. Like huge. Seven hundred million dollars or some ridiculous number like that. And you can't buy a Powerball ticket in Nevada, we don't actually have lotteries here because… well, who knows why. So people get in the car, drive to California, and buy tickets. Then if they win, they have to pick their money up across state lines. It's dumb, but whatever.

So I was in the grocery store while all this Powerball mania was going on and the woman in front of me must've known the checker because they gabbed for a good seven minutes about what they were gonna do with their money if they won.

Buy big houses, fancy cars, go to Europe, put all their kids through college. Shit like that. And I remember thinking, "I honestly have no clue what I would do with money like that if I won."

And now I have won, and this is what I'm doing.

I'm tempted to feel proud, but then I remember that this is how Scotty lived his whole life. In service to something greater than himself. And he never once asked for a pat on the back. He just did what he thought was right. And while I'll probably never be as un-selfish and noble as my brother, I can at least try for the "not being proud of myself" part.

Tyler is gone right now. On his way to talk with Dr. Eldridge about how he's cured—I have to chuckle, because that's how he's been phrasing this visit. He's "cured." So I'm here alone. And this house, man... it's something else. Huge, like so many bedrooms, and so many living rooms and more than one kitchen—three, if you count the outdoor one—and more bathrooms than two people need. Like every bedroom has a bathroom.

And this place is super cool, but only if the house is full.

Right now, it feels pretty empty.

I can imagine nothing worse than getting everything you ever wanted and having no one to share it with.

So yeah, I won the Powerball alright, but my prize wasn't Tyler's money.

It was Tyler.

And if I ever lost him... God. That hurts to even think about. But if I ever lost him... no amount of money could ever make me feel better. A huge pool with real rock landscaping would not replace him. Having an equal number of bathrooms to bedrooms would not make up for my loss.

Money isn't everything. I thought it was, but I was wrong.

Life is about purpose. And if I'm being generous with myself, I'd say that's what I was really looking for when I came up with all those crazy ideas to make money. It wasn't the paycheck I needed, but the purpose.

In fact, I have no desire to buy anything right now. Not that it's my money, but I could very easily ask Tyler for things and he'd just go get them for me. Fancy purse. Done. Diamond necklace. Done. New luxury car. Done.

But if he tries to do that—and I don't think he would because I think we have a similar worldview about this—I'm gonna say no.

I'll say it gently, because if he ever did get it in his head to go out and start buying me shit, there'd be a reason for it. But I don't want any of that *stuff*.

I just want to be with him. I want him to be safe, and healthy, and happy. That's it. That's all I need.

My phone is in the bedroom, so I get up from the pool and go get it. I find Plumeria Brown's contact, press send, and get her voicemail.

I decide what I have to say can be said on a voicemail.

"Hey, Plu. Maddie Clayton here. No need to call me back, there's no emergency. I just wanted to call and say... thank you." I smile into my phone. "Yeah, that's pretty much it. Just thank you. And hey, maybe we'll see each other sometime. Like when there's no crisis or anything. You, know. As friends and shit."

I press end on the phone and walk back out to the pool. I like the pool, not because it's hot out or anything, but because the waterfall makes noise. It's just too quiet in that house. It's just too big. It's just... not me.

And then I'm pressing another contact and when my mom answers and says, "Maddie? What's wrong?" I feel a stab of guilt. Because she automatically assumes I'm in trouble. And the reason she assumes that is because I never call her, and when I do, I usually am calling to ask for something. Money mostly.

"Nothing, Mom."

"But you're calling me."

"I know," I say, trying to laugh it off. "But I swear, nothing's wrong. In fact, I have good news."

I have this sudden need to tell my mother I'm happy. And the words just come out, the same way they did when I was talking to Scotty.

"So Tyler and I are together..."

And I go on, and on, and on. I tell her nothing bad, even though most of what we've done in the past couple months has been kin-da cra-zy. I tell her about the date to the Hoover Dam, minus the tunnel stuff, of course. And I tell her about his makeover with Rodney, and how good he looks, and send her a picture that I took last night on my phone. And my mom makes a big deal about it, and us, and I swear to God, I don't think she's been this happy in years. Maybe since Scotty died.

So when that chat is over I go there. "We went to see Scotty," I say. And I tell her about that. And she is quiet, and I talk softer, and we are both crying before I'm done.

But it's the kind of cry that's OK, ya know? It's the kind of cry that says, *I got through it. It was hard, and it took a long time, but I'm still here.*

And before I know it, my phone is dying and I say, "I gotta go," because I figure we've been talking long enough.

But she says, "Go find your charger."

And I don't even argue. I go find it, and we talk more. And my dad gets on the phone, and we make plans for Tyler and me to come see them.

And even though I've resisted that every time they've said it before—why, I'm not really sure. Maybe because I'd have to admit that they'd moved on and I was still stuck—I don't resist now. I actually daydream about it.

And when we hang up, I feel happy.

I feel peaceful for the first time in seven years.

I feel, to use Tyler's words, cured.

147

CHAPTER FIFTEEN

TYLER

Sitting down on the sofa in Dr. Eldridge's shrink-house, it strikes me that the place looks brighter. It's always been nice and warm and inviting, but it just seems cheerier somehow.

"Did you paint in here?" I ask.

She presses her lips together in a moment of consideration, the way people do when you've managed to make them question for a fraction of a second something they already know to be fact. Then she shakes her head and says, "No."

"Huh." I nod, looking around. "Seems sunnier."

She puts on one of her kind, sweet, Dr. Eldridge smiles and says, "You shaved."

"Oh. Yeah. Well, I didn't, actually. Rodney's the name of the guy who shaved me, but yeah. The beard came off."

She nods a little. "How's it feel?"

"Uh, good. Weird. Good and weird." I decide not to tell her that when my skin touches Maddie's mouth or pussy or asshole that it feels like getting my very first teenage blowjob over and over again every time. That moment of, "How is this a feeling that I haven't ever had

149

before?" I mean, the doc's cool and all, but I don't need to be telling her all about my oral fixation.

"So," she says. "What's going on? In your message you said you think you're cured?"

"Oh, yeah. I mean, that was... y'know, that was kind of a joke. You got that it was a joke, right?"

"No, I just figured I'm that good at my job."

She's so fucking awesome.

"Ha! Yeah. Well, I mean you are, but... I just wanted to get together one last time to say thank you for everything."

Maybe I'm misreading it, but there's something I flag as sadness flashing across her face.

"Are you going somewhere?" she asks.

"Um, yeah. I mean, eventually. But just for right now I'm going to kind of just... be. Just wherever I am. With Maddie." I can feel myself smiling. I probably look like a dope. I don't care.

She gets a tiny smile too, but only around the corners of her eyes. "So that's working out?"

"Yeah. Yeah. It is."

She lifts her eyebrows. "OK. Great."

"Hey," I tell her, "I'm as fucking surprised as anybody. But it is. It's great. She's amazing."

"I'm so glad. And she's OK? I mean I heard about the fire at Pete's Strip Club."

"Oh, you did?"

"I did. Pete's Strip Club, off the Strip. Where Maddie was stripping."

"Ha! You remember that. She's... She's fine. Thanks."

"The owner, Pete? He passed away in the fire?"

I take a deep breath and let it out on the word, "Yeah."

"I'm sorry. Did you know him?"

"Uh... little bit. Yeah."

"I am sorry. Did they find out what happened?"

Jesus. I didn't anticipate this. And I want to tell her the truth. I really do. I want to tell her all of it. I don't know why, I just do. But I'm not sure exactly how elastic the boundaries of our patient confidentiality are, so I say, "Electrical."

She considers this, then says, "And so coming out of that, and particularly with what you had just gone through together, you and Maddie are still...?"

"Oh. Oh. Yeah, I get what you're saying, but it's not co-dependent or, like, born out of guilt or trauma or anything fucked up like that."

"OK. And just so you know, I didn't presume that it was."

"No, I know, but I just felt like I should say it."

"K. And how do you feel? Having said it?"

That's my favorite thing about Doc Eldridge. She doesn't just let me get away with shit. She's always challenging me to figure out *why* I'm doing or saying something. I mean, I should be clear...I like it *now*. It also had the ability to drive me crazy for a while. But, in the place I am at the moment, I kinda dig it.

"Uh..." I think. "How do I feel? I feel like I'm not talking bullshit. Like this is all what I really, truly, deeply believe."

"Well, great then. Because that's kind of the part that matters."

"Yeah. Ain't it just?"

I make a tight-lipped smile and nod my head for a good ten seconds. She tilts her head forward, smiles back, raises her eyebrows and asks, "What else?"

"Oh. We went to Scotty's grave. Or, I mean, I went for the first time. But we went together."

"Her brother."

"Yeah."

"And? How was it?"

"Um..." My inclination is to say, "good," or "hard," or, "hard but good," or some other version of that shit. And while any of it would be true, it's also inadequate. "It was... a start," I say. "I mean, I have lots of feelings about it, but the truth is it just felt like a pretty good start."

The smile on her face now is maybe the most genuine I've ever seen from her. "Good," she says. "And what comes next?"

"You mean like, in general or...?"

"Whichever." She shrugs.

"Well, um, long-term... You remember me telling you about Nadir?"

"Your friend who died?"

"Yeah. I told you about what he had wanted to do whenever we got paid for the thing we invented?"

"Remind me?"

"Just... good shit. Like friggin' Mother Teresa shit. Like philanthropy and stuff. Notably, he wanted to build schools for girls in Afghanistan."

She nods yet again. "That's noble."

"Yeah, no shit. So I think that's what we're gonna do. Me and Maddie. Go help do the work Nadir would've wanted. I'm gonna try to find his family first. See if they need anything. But then, yeah... doing good deeds and whatnot."

"Well, that's wonderful. And Maddie is excited about this too?"

"Yeah. Yeah, she is. That's the thing. We're kind of in exactly the same place. Well, not *exactly*, we're two different people. I can't know *exactly* where anyone else is in their own head, right?"

She laughs a little and looks pleased, like you do with a kid who's been staring at the same goddamn math problem for a really long time and finally figures out that two plus two equals four. Then she says, "Right."

"Right. But we're in similar places, I think, in terms of what we want out of our lives. And I think both of us feel like helping other people is a not-asshole way to spend the next however long. I mean, we're lucky as fuck, and I'm not sure either one of us feels like we deserve how lucky we are. So maybe this will make us feel a little better about everything. Which is still just kind of another way of being selfish, I guess. But, y'know. Baby steps."

She laughs again. "Will that be dangerous? Building schools, especially for girls, in Afghanistan?"

"Probably. I can't imagine ever doing anything that's not hugely unnecessarily dangerous, but y'know, you can take the boy out of the battle-zone, but..." She looks a little concerned. "I'm kidding! I'm joking! But, I mean, yeah, of course, it's gonna be crazy dangerous. But if the government wants to keep using the tech Nadir and I invented, they'll have to give us some cover or whatever. I mean, we're not just gonna charge in there blindly without both being properly prepared and with all the backup we need and so forth." *Not again. Tried that. Shit doesn't work great.* "So it's all gonna be above board and thoughtful and... Don't worry. I'll be OK." I say the last bit because she looks genuinely concerned.

"I'm not worried," she suggests.

"Awww, c'mon, Doc. You know you love me the best. I'm your favorite client. Don't lie. You'd be all busted up if something bad happened. You can admit it." I lean in, smile, nudge my elbow in her direction, and wink.

She rests her cheek on her hand. "What else?"

"Oh, I dunno. Nothing really."

"Any plans for New Year's?" she asks.

Huh. That's right. New Year's Eve is tomorrow. With everything we've been through and been dealing with, I don't think either of us have taken the chance to even think much at all about "celebrating." This new year doesn't feel like that. Even though there is obviously a lot to celebrate when you get right down to it. But it feels more like turning a page. A quiet turn. A gentle pivoting. As opposed to some cataclysmic new ending or new beginning. Yeah. We've definitely had enough of those.

Although I do keep getting those texts saying, "Big plans for the New Year?" Somebody's definitely trying to get me excited to go to whatever party or shindig they're promoting. I am still tempted to text back STOP, but I'm restraining myself. They won't lure me in. Fucking telemarketers.

"No," I say. "No plans. Not really." Then I remember. "Oh. There is one thing, kinda."

"What's that?"

"Um, well, not for tomorrow night or whatever, but later today. I'm, uh, I'm sitting down with my dad for the first time since I was eighteen."

Dr. Eldridge is too good at her job to betray her composure, but she does take an elongated breath before saying, "Really?"

"Yeah. Yep. Yes, indeed."

"How'd that come to pass?"

"Fuckin' destiny, I suppose."

"What does that mean?"

"Means I ran into him by accident and then after that, the guy came looking for me. So, I figure that something's trying to say we should hook up, so we are."

"Where are you meeting?"

"Frank's. You know Frank's?"

She nods. "And..."

"And what? And how do I feel about it and whatever?" She nods again. "Not sure. Curious, I suppose."

"Sure. About what exactly?"

I take a moment to contemplate about what exactly. Because I'm not even completely sure I know. "Oh, I guess more than anything, I wanna see if I even still know the guy anymore. I mean, shit, like, he was one way for a long time, and then my mom died, and he became this totally other, really horrible fucking way, and that's how I remember him, but that's not happening *now*, right?"

She doesn't say anything, just keeps watching me.

"I mean, fuck, Doc, look at me just in the time you've known me. Do I seem like the same guy?"

"Yes. But the same guy with perhaps an evolving worldview."

So fuckin' literal.

"OK, sure. But I suppose I feel like if I can see that kind of thing happening in myself, isn't it possible that it could happen in my dad? And maybe if some of the guy I remember, who I liked, is still there, then maybe we can... I dunno. I'm just curious. OK? That's all."

I cross my arms and feel my shoulders rising a little to my ears. I'm not sure why I feel defensive. Or maybe I do. I think it's because she's asking me to explain in words a feeling that might be inexplicable. Which is not her fault. It's her job. But it's making my throat itch.

"I think it's great that you're going to see your dad," she says. Then adds, "If that's what you want."

"It is." I tell her. "It is what I want." *I think.*

"Can I give you a suggestion?"

That's weird. She's never offered me a suggestion before. She'll make, like, observations, and offer "thoughts," but she's never come right out before and given me advice.

"Uh... sure."

"Or maybe just a tool you can choose to use if you feel it might serve you at all."

"OK."

"If possible, see if you can distance yourself from the interaction."

"I don't... What does that mean?"

She swallows and starts again. "If you can, try to step outside yourself and engage with your dad on two levels. The first level being the you that's sitting there talking with him, and the second level being that of a reporter."

"So... you want me to encourage a split personality? Because that seems like a real step backwards, Doc. No offense."

She closes her eyes and takes a breath. "I know it sounds weird and may not even be something that you're able to do, but if you can, allow yourself to be an observer who's chronicling the interaction. Who's assembling notes for reportage to you later."

"Oooo-kay," I say.

"I know, I know, it sounds weird. But look at it this way: Our brains are usually doing two things at once anyway, yes? Being present where we are, but at the same time, most of us are thinking a hundred other thoughts simultaneously."

"No idea what you're talking about."

She takes the most indiscernible of moments to acknowledge my wittiness and then goes on.

"So, all I'm suggesting is that you take that companion track that's running in your brain and put it to use. Allow yourself the opportunity to observe and report on everything that goes on with your dad. I'm just trying to give you a chance to be there and at the same time have a clinical remove from the environment so that your emotions – good or bad – don't overtake the moment. Thus the reporter metaphor."

I get what she's saying. It's not a terrible idea. I'm just worried that I might not be able to pull it off. "Should I wear a little reporter hat and carry a steno pad? Because I feel like that would really complete the look."

"It's just a suggestion. If it doesn't feel useful, feel free to disregard."

"Sorry, I didn't mean to be a dick."

She smiles a genuine and authentic, toothy grin. "You weren't."

I take a moment to consider what she's telling me. "Reporter, huh?"

"A way of seeing the events as separate from the feelings about the events."

I blow my lips out. "Yeah. That makes... it's not stupid."

"I hope not. I try to give my favorite clients the not-stupid suggestions."

For real. The greatest. I may just keep in touch with her anyway, even though I'm cured and shit. She's rad.

"What if I brought Maddie with me?" I ask.

"Um... I mean, if you'd like to bring her, I mean, sure. Were you not going to?"

"Nah. I mean, my dad knows her from before and I'd have to explain and—"

"No, you wouldn't."

"I wouldn't?"

"Tyler." She leans in a fraction of an inch. "Of all the things I know about you, one of them is that you are not a person who does things because they *have* to."

She allows that to land and I don't bother to pick it up. Neither does she. We both just let it sit there.

"I may bring her with me," I finally say.

"Yeah?"

"Yeah. I mean, she's a part of my life now. Again. Now and again, I guess. So, if we're gonna...whatever, I'd like to start now. I suppose. Also, if I get distracted and forget to take notes or whatever, she can be my backup. Maybe I'll see if she'll wear like a little pencil skirt and glasses and put her hair in a bun and stuff. Because that'll make it all easier no matter what. So that'll be good."

Dr. Eldridge gestures with her hands in a, "you do you, boo," manner. (I know that's not her intention, but it's the effect.) "OK," she says. "Anything else then that you want to talk about?"

I take a second in this moment to reflect on how far and how fast things have gone for me since Maddie came back into my life. Since we came back into each other's lives. I know the doc would hasten to point out that Maddie's not responsible for what's happened in my life in these last couple of months and that if I'm sitting in a better place in the world it's owed to me and my work on me above all. And she'd argue the same for Maddie. And she'd be right, of course.

But still...

Doctor Eldridge can't argue against the fact that in order to start our own, individual races, we all need a trigger. An impetus. An inspiration. Something that kicks us in the ass and *compels* us to change, or to discover ourselves in a new way, or to *want* to even try. And if the starting pistol comes in the form of another person, so be it.

Some people find a hobby, like rock climbing or skydiving. Some people take up painting or sculpture. Some people find religion. Whatever. Maddie and I found each other. And inside of the other we found the missing parts of ourselves. And it shouldn't be weird that that's where we were hiding. We were part of each other's evolution as people from way before now. We are in each other's DNA.

"No," I say. "No. Honestly, I think I'm... good. Like, actually OK. You remember back when you said that you thought I created stuff that would keep me in conflict? You know, so that I would always have something to fight against?"

"I do."

"Well, I don't feel like I wanna do that anymore. I mean, I know there'll still be times when I'll have to fight. Let's just face facts, that's the way the world is."

"It can be."

"Yeah. It can. But what I suppose I've decided is that that shit is hard enough. It doesn't need my help. So I'm done fighting just for the sake of fighting."

She eyes me and then cocks her head and says, "Can I ask you something?"

"Sure."

After a long, long, long moment she says, "Do you feel like you won?"

I take a few beats to think about what that implies. What it means to win. The cost of winning. The price of being a victor. If your hand is raised in triumph, someone else's is lowered in defeat. Do I want to be a vanquisher? Do I want to be triumphant? Do I even *want* to win?

At what cost, victory?

So. Considering all that, I choose my words carefully when I finally answer.

"No," I say, slowly. "But I guess... I feel like I didn't lose."

CHAPTER SIXTEEN

MADDIE

When we pull up to Caroline and Diane's, I feel a little, tiny bit weird. Because I can't pretend I live here anymore. I just don't. And I won't. Ever again. And I feel really good about that. But the more good I feel, and the more things seem like they're going my way, the more I worry about Caroline and Diane. I'm not trying to infantilize them. They're grown women, not kids, but still. I do worry about them.

We're swinging by because we're sort of near anyway as we head to see Tyler's dad. I was surprised that he asked me to come with him, but really touched by the request. Just like I told Mom and Dad about me and Tyler, I think he wants to tell his parent about us too. He didn't say that, and I doubt he ever would. He just talked about Dr. Eldridge and reporter's hats and stuff, but I think there's a part of him that wants to introduce his girlfriend to his folks. Because he's probably never done anything like that.

The pretense under which we're at my old house is to bring Diane and Caroline a bottle of champagne. There's a liquor store nearby and as we were passing it, Tyler suddenly pulled into the parking lot and said, "Let's bring Caroline and Diane something for New Year's!"

I asked him why and he talked again about having been kind of a jerk to whichever one he was a jerk to – he still can't remember for sure which one it was – and about what he and I talked about with wanting to help them somehow, and how they were good friends to me, and stuff like that. And that's all nice, and possibly even true, but the real reason we're making a pit stop is because he's nervous about seeing Jack. I'm already starting to know these things about him without him having to tell me.

We hop out of the Tesla and walk up to the front door. It looks like they're both here. Both of their cars are parked outside. I'm holding the champagne bottle and as we land on the front steps, I am suddenly overcome with the strange impulse to ring the bell. Because it's not my house. I'm a visitor. A tourist. And my polite impulses take over. But in a split second I decide that it would be way, way more uncool to declare myself as someone who's apart from this place than to just walk through the damn door like I have every other time before, so I pull out my key and put it in the lock.

"Hey!" I say brightly into the room as the door opens. And here's what we see as we cross the threshold: Caroline is sitting on the sofa, hunched over a laptop. Diane is pacing behind her, tapping on a bottle of beer with her ringed index finger, which is causing a clicking sound. Both of them look incredibly focused and neither one responds to our arrival.

"Read it back?" says Diane.

Caroline fans up on the laptop's track pad and says, "'Agatha, Christie, Deborah, and Mona. Three call girls and a stripper. That's what they were. Christie and Deborah looked at each other and their shared expression told the story. 'How did we get here?' Neither one of them said anything aloud. They didn't have to. They both knew. It was time. Time for something to change.'"

I turn to look at Tyler and he shrugs at me, raising his eyebrows.

Diane takes a sip of her beer. "I dunno. It feels clunky."

"You think?" says Caroline. "I like it."

"It's kind of the seminal moment. It needs to have impact. Gravitas."

"I agree. That's why I broke it up into short sentences. To punctuate it."

"Yeah," Diane says, taking another sip, "just something..." Then she looks over and sees me and Tyler, seemingly for the first time. "Oh. Hey," she says. "What are you doing here?"

"Um," I say, offering the champagne, "we wanted to bring you guys this for New Year's."

"Aww. That's so sweet. Thanks!" says Caroline, standing up and reaching for the bottle. Then she sees what it is and says, "Guys... really? This is like a four-hundred-dollar bottle of champagne."

If there's one thing strippers and call-girls know about, it's how much expensive booze costs.

"Oh, yeah, well..." I say, suddenly kind of ashamed about it.

"Thanks," says Diane, stepping over and taking it from Caroline. "Appreciate it."

She manages to be both genuinely gracious in her thanks and kind of cold about it all at the same time. Which is an amazing skill and I wonder if she knows it's her superpower.

"What are you guys doing?" I ask.

They share a furtive look with each other. Caroline tilts her head in a 'should we?" way. Diane shakes her head in a 'no' way. Then Caroline's eyes widen in a 'come on' way. And finally, Diane just outright says, "Fine," and turns with the champagne to place it on a side table.

"We're working on our memoir," Caroline says with a shrug.

"Your memoir?" I ask.

"Yeah," says Caroline. "We quit our other job."

"You did?" I don't know if the surprise or the excitement is what comes through more in my voice, but both are certainly present.

"Yeah, we did," says Diane, stepping back over. "So that we can work full time on this."

"Yeah. And also because, you know, our jobs were..." Caroline trails off.

"Sleeping with people for money sucks. Bad," Diane says, and then takes another swig of her beer.

Then Caroline looks past me and says, "Tyler?"

"Hey, uh... Car-o-line?" He draws it out and kind of makes it a question. I close my eyes and shake my head the tiniest bit.

"Wow," she says. "You shaved." And then she gets sort of self-conscious. It's sweet. On most other women it would be out of place and the kind of thing that might raise my ire without me being able to help it, but you just gotta love Caroline.

"I didn't," he says. "Rodney shaved me, but..." I look over my shoulder at him and he stops and just says, "Thanks."

"So now you're just...?" I start to ask.

Diane says, "We're gonna work on the memoir. We're just gonna bang it out. We figure we have probably enough saved to get us by for two, three months. So we're gonna do this and see if we can sell it. If you're worried, don't be. We've changed everybody's names." She says that last part kind of snarky.

"I wasn't worried," I say, quietly.

"You're Mona now," Caroline offers. "I'm Christie, Diane's Deborah, and Annie is Agatha."

"Wow," I say. "Have you talked to Annie?"

"About the book?" Diane asks. "Yeah, she thinks it's awesome." She takes another swig from the bottle.

"Oh. Cool. But I meant, just, how's she doing?"

"She seems great," Diane says, her voice ringed around the edges with annoyance. "She's terrific. Everybody's doing great. So. Thanks for stopping by and for the champagne and yeah. Thanks. See ya."

She turns and makes for the kitchen. I'm about to say something, but before I can, it's Tyler's voice that stops her.

"How are you guys gonna get it published?"

"What?" Diane asks, turning around and glaring. Tyler finally told me the story of what happened last week. How he got all angry at her and how she seemed scared. So I don't blame her. I'd still be pissed too.

"Do you guys have a publisher or an agent or...? I'm just curious."

"We're just gonna self-publish it," says Caroline. "One of the girls we work with—"

"Used to work with," Diane interrupts.

"Right, *used* to work with, um, she loves romance novels? And she told us that independently published romance novels are like the biggest sector of the publishing industry."

"Really?" I say. I don't know why I find that surprising. I just do.

"Yeah," she goes on. "These writers, some of them do really well. And, well, we both took some creative writing courses in school, and we figured that we could probably just give it a shot. But then we decided... y'know, our real-life story is also probably just as interesting—"

"More," says Diane.

"Yeah, maybe more," Caroline continues, "and it's a crazy story. Four girls who all graduated from college together with degrees and stuff and we all became..." She trails off and bites her lip. "I mean... we just think it's a good story."

"Wow," I say again, "That's... That's amazing. Congrats, you guys."

"Thanks," says Diane. "We do have degrees in fuckin' econ. We should be able to figure out how to grab some of the co-ed-turned-prostitute-turned-memoirist market share. It can't be that glutted."

Was that a joke? I think Diane may actually just have cracked a joke.

"Um..." That's Tyler's voice again. "Can I help?"

All three of us look at him.

"What?" asks Caroline. "Help us write it?"

"Oh. No. God, no. I just... I know a guy. A guy in New York from when I was living there. Good dude. He's an editor at one of the major publishing houses."

"Which one?" asks Diane.

"Um... Tran-ton-feld?"

Diane and Caroline look at each other. "That's not a thing," Diane says.

"Oh. Well, one of 'em. I know it's a good one because dude has a sick apartment. I can call him and ask which." Tyler goes to pull out his phone.

"No. No. That's fine," says Diane. And there's a beat while Caroline and Diane – Diane mostly – try to size up how full of shit they think Tyler is. "Go on," she says.

"I dunno. I mean, I can give him a shout and ask him to take a read of it when you're done. If you're interested," he says. "But if you wanna go this other route, that's fine too, just trying to give options."

Tyler sighs. I love him so much right now. Not because he's trying to do a nice thing, but because it's clearly hard and awkward, and I know how he feels. It's one thing to make all these great, philanthropic, altruistic plans. It's another thing to put them into motion. Or even to really know how to start. This is a start. This is a way we can help Diane and Caroline.

We can encourage them.

We can foster their ambitions and encourage them to try. We don't have to ride in on a white horse and save the day. We can just be supportive friends. At the end of the day, that's what Raven did for me, even if I had no idea she was doing it, and even if, at the time, it looked nothing even remotely like generosity... that's what it was. And offering to give somebody hope, which is what Tyler's doing right now, sometimes that's all a person needs.

"And also, if you guys want to take some extra time to make sure it's really, really perfect so you can slam-dunk it, I can bankroll you while you do that."

And sometimes you can offer to give someone a whole shitload of fucking money. That's another way to help people, I guess.

"What?" asks Diane with a sharpness in her tone.

"I just mean... if this is something you really want to do and really care about and believe in, you shouldn't have to just bang it out and hope for the best. You should be able to take your time with it, and make it great, and all that shit. Right? I mean, this is *your* story. I imagine you'd wanna make it as perfect as possible." No one says anything as we all process this offer he's making. "But shit. Fuck do I know? I ain't never made anything. Except messes. And I do that for free."

There's another long beat where Caroline looks back at Diane. Diane doesn't make eye contact, just keeps staring at Tyler.

"Whatayou get?" she asks.

"What?" says Ty.

"We gave up the whore business. That's what this whole thing's about. We're not interested in working for another pimp."

"Oh!" he says. "Oh, God. No. No, of course. Of course not. I just..." He takes a breath. "I want to help you. That's what I want. That's what I get out of it. Helping somebody."

"Why?" Diane asks, suspiciously.

I look at him and touch him on the arm. "Because you helped me," I tell her. Which is only part of the story, but it's not bullshit.

"Yeah," says Tyler. "Yeah. I'd be like your patron. Like in Elizabethan England and shit, didn't playwrights and stuff have patrons? Rich assholes who paid for Shakespeare and Marlowe and all those guys to just write? Without having to worry about day jobs and shit? Just for the sake of feeling like they were doing something important even though they had no talent themselves?

168

Well... I'm a rich, talentless asshole. Lemme be your patron. Please?"

I'll take issue with one thing Tyler just said. He may be rich, and he may be an asshole, but he is not talentless. His talent is persuasion. And that pitch was just about as persuasive as it could be.

Caroline looks excitedly and expectantly at Diane. Diane continues just looking at Tyler. Her left knee bounces where she stands.

"And you don't want shit in return?"

He shakes his head. "Just for you to do the best with it you can." She starts to nod. "And maybe a thanks in the credits if it gets made into a movie." Her eyes dart up to meet his again. "Or not. Either way. No problem."

She puts both hands in front of her lips in a prayer position, her left knee still juddering in place. After a long moment, she finally says...

"K."

"K?" he repeats.

"K," she says. "It's the least you can do after being a dick the way you were."

"Agreed," says Tyler.

"Well, OK then!" chirps Caroline.

"Um... OK then," I say.

"So..." Diane starts.

"Champagne?" asks Tyler. "Toast the adventure?"

Diane smirks a little and says, "Sure."

She grabs the bottle off the side table and carries it into the kitchen. Caroline starts to come give Tyler a hug, then stops, then starts again, then stops, and then finally Tyler just reaches down and hugs her instead.

"Thank you," I hear her whisper.

"Glad to be able to do it," he says. And glad is the right word.

We should all be glad.

Caroline trots off to the kitchen as well and I turn to Tyler, wrap my arms around his neck and say, "I love you."

"Yeah?"

"Yeah." I smile.

"Thank fucking God, because I love the daylights out of you." We kiss. And then he says, "Fuck."

"What? What's wrong?"

"I sure hope they don't suck. This was very impulsive."

I smile and take him by the hand into the kitchen where Diane is finishing pouring the expensive champagne into four water glasses.

"To new beginnings!" Caroline says.

Yeah. To new beginnings.

I will definitely drink to that.

And then we all lift our glasses to the sky. And we do.

CHAPTER SEVENTEEN

TYLER

Pulling up to Frank's feels like a collision of past and present. Frank's itself is something out of a time capsule. I don't know if it was actually built in the fifties or if it was built as a nostalgic homage, but either way, it harkens back to a bygone era in Vegas. An era of shiny suits and hair gel. Of people dressing up for a night out on the town. Of the Rat Pack. All that shit. But here it still sits. A little older, a little more run-down, but still going.

When I was a shorty, we'd swing in here on Saturdays as our "Saturday thing." After Little League games, win or lose, me, Mom, and Jack would stop in for milkshakes. Frank's is where I learned about a Black and White. It was Mom's flavor. Chocolate and vanilla swirled together and poured into a tall, ridged tumbler.

This is the kind of joint where they also slap down on the table the metal container they used to make the shake itself. So that when you've consumed all the creamy dairy goodness in your glass and can't possibly take in one more sip, you still feel like you have to give it a shot. And then you lift that frosty, condensation-ringed metal to your mouth, polish off the contents, and throw up all over the table.

171

(OK. It only happened the once, but it's the memory that sticks with me. I mean, shit, I was seven, gimme a break.)

And just like Frank's, here I still sit. A little older, a little more run-down, but still going, too.

OK. Let's do this thing.

I glance at the clock on the Tesla's massive computer screen (the car itself is actually just a computer on wheels, which makes me wonder what the fuck happens if it gets hacked) and see that it's three fifty-five. I look around the parking lot, but realize that I have no idea what kind of car my dad drives, so I wouldn't know if he's here or not. But through the windows, I don't see him inside, so I guess we're here first.

"How you doing?" Maddie's voice pulls my attention back to now.

"Fine. Good. Too good, really. How's it with you, Pop-Tart?" I know that I'm overdoing it with the charm offensive, but I don't care. I kind of don't want to hide that I'm nervous. I figure if I can't be real when I'm with Maddie then when the fuck can I be? And I'm tired of not being honest about my feelings. There's enough in my life to make me tired, I don't need to add to that shit.

"Yeah," she says, "you seem *too* good." She smiles and rubs her hand on my arm.

"Thanks for coming with me," I say and then blow out a breath.

"Hey, I go where you go."

She winks, and I take my whole hand and spread my palm out over her face. "I fuckin' love you. I just wanna crush your head."

"Yeah, well, that's love, I suppose."

I don't crush her head. Instead, I take my hand away, lean over, and give her a kiss that's half-want, half-need. She moans a little.

My lips still on hers, I say, "You wanna blow this off and just go... I dunno...."

"Fuck?" she mutters back.

"Capital idea!" I say, hitting the ignition button and popping the car into reverse.

She presses the park button and turns the car off. "Later. Promise," she says.

I make a plane propeller sound with my tongue, nod my head, and say, "OK. Fuck. Let's get our reporter hats on."

Stepping out of the car, I can smell Frank's. It's that burger and fry smell emanating from the kitchen's exhaust fan out into the desert air. It makes me immediately hungry. I don't think I've eaten today. I've been that preoccupied with this whole get-together. I stroll to the door and pull it open, holding it for Maddie.

"Why, thank you, kind sir," she says.

"M'lady," I offer back along with a deep bow at the waist and a flourish of my hand. Seriously, I would've been a fucking baller in Elizabethan England. Probably woulda been an earl or some shit. Maybe I was. I should get a past-life reading from one of those fortune tellers who work out of their houses and find out. Anyway.

I look around one more time just to see if Dad is here. I don't spy him, but I do spy that our booth is open, so I point to it and Maddie nods and heads over.

"You wanna sit across from each other or same side?" she asks.

"Um... whichever, I guess."

She plops into the booth, onto the side facing the entrance. The vinyl seat squeaks a tiny bit as she slides over next to the window. She pats the space beside her and says, "C'mere." I do. I slide in next to her. She says, "Tactical. We're facing the door, we're both on the same side so it's two against one, and you have the exit position in the event shit gets hot and you need to scramble."

I stare at her for a beat and blink twice. "You totally didn't need my help down in Mexico, did you?"

"Not really. But I was glad to see you anyway."

The waitress approaches. She's probably in her early forties, mousy blonde hair, thin, pretty. Her name tag says "Victoria." She hands us menus.

"You guys waiting on somebody?"

"Uh, yeah," I say. "But we can go ahead and get started. You hungry, babe?" I ask Maddie. She nods. "Yeah, so, um we'll take a look, but can you bring us a Black and White while we figure it out?"

"Starting with dessert. My kinda people," she says on a smile. She smiles like a showgirl. Who knows? Maybe she was. "I'll be back. Take your time," she says, and heads off.

I glance at the clock on my phone. Four o'clock. I start biting unconsciously at my bottom lip. I know that I am because Maddie asks, "Still OK?"

"Yeah, yeah. Why?"

"Because you're chewing on your lips. Although you could just be really hungry."

I stop biting at my bottom lip. "I'm fine."

"Look at it this way... If you see him and decide that you don't want to do this after all, we can probably slip out. You shaved. There's a totally reasonable chance he won't recognize you."

I start smiling despite myself. "You really went there with that joke, didn't you?"

She shrugs and grins. "I learned from the best."

Victoria returns with our shake. "Here you go. One Black and White and two straws." She puts the glass with the creamy confection down on the table, and then, as remembered, she places the metal mixing container with the remainder down as well. "You guys think you're ready to order anything, or you still wanna wait?"

I glance at Maddie who says, "We'll go ahead and get something now. I'm starving." I love that Maddie's always hungry. I don't know why. It just makes me happy. "Can I get a cheeseburger, no lettuce?"

"You want fries or a salad?"

"Fries. Gotta carb-load. I'll probably work out later." She nudges me in the ribs. "How 'bout you?" she asks me.

"Um, same. Thanks."

"You got it."

We hand Victoria back the menus and she heads off again.

"The carb-loading joke was solid, huh?" Maddie asks. She's trying to keep my mind from wandering too far and keep me in "reporter" mode. And I appreciate it. I really do. But I'm having a tough time.

I try to do what Doc Eldridge said though. Step apart from myself. Observe what's happening. Catalogue the moment. But it's tough, because it's now a couple minutes past the time Jack and I were supposed to meet and the only people sitting here in this booth are me and Maddie.

She must be able to read my thoughts because she says, "He'll be here. I know he will."

"Yeah? How?"

"Dunno. Just one of those things."

175

She takes the flexible straws, one by one, bends them at the neck, and places them in the milkshake.

"Here," she says. "Drink this with me. We can stare into each other's eyes and bump heads and giggle and shit. It'll be adorable."

I love her more and more every goddamn second.

"OK," I say, forcing out a laugh. I place my mouth around the straw just as she does and we both sip.

Swallowing, she pulls her mouth away and says, "Holy shit, that's good."

"Yeah," I agree.

"Is it as good as you remember?"

I look at her. She wears an expression of hopeful expectancy. Her eyes are wide, and her lips are puckered as she finishes swallowing the slurp of milky goodness. She is a waking dream. My waking dream.

"Better," I tell her.

Victoria approaches the table.

"All done?" she asks.

Maddie has finished almost her whole plate of food. I've only kind of picked at mine. Most of my fries are still there and there are a few bites out of my burger. My napkin sits crumpled on top of the plate of partially eaten food.

"Yeah, yeah, I think we're done," says Maddie.

"Anything else?" Victoria asks, cautiously. I imagine being a waitress at a diner in Vegas you learn to read people pretty well. And I'm making no attempt to hide the way I feel right now, so she's got to be picking up the energy that's wafting off the table.

"Just the check, thanks," Maddie responds. Victoria nods and heads off.

It's starting to get dark outside. I look at the time on my phone again. Five o'clock.

Five o'clock.

Ladies and gentlemen, we have a breaking story on today's five o'clock news. In what should come as a shock to no one, Jack Morgan, father to Tyler Morgan, following a long history of being a terrible fucking parent, continues his nearly unbroken record of failing to execute the most basic example of what it might mean to be someone's dad, or even a decent person, for that matter. There will be no film at eleven, because there's nothing to fucking show. In the weather, storm clouds are imminent.

"I'm sorry, Ty," Maddie says.

I don't even try to pretend. "Me too." I hang my head and shake it a tiny bit. I don't even really feel that sad. I just feel...stupid. Which, I suppose, is something I should be fucking used to by now, but it never gets any more fun. I blow my lips out and make an attempt to rally. "All good," I say. "Let's go. You ate an assload of fries. We gotta go work that shit off."

I slap the Formica tabletop with my hand, slide out of the booth and stand, turning to offer my hand to Maddie as I do. I am the Fifth Earl of Dumbfuckery.

She's just about to her feet when I hear, "Christ! Ty! You shaved! Jeez Louise, ya look like a fuckin' million bucks!"

And I turn to see... Jack Morgan.

A very drunk Jack Morgan.

His tie is loose. His hair is messed up. His shirt is half-untucked from his pants. His fucking fly is down. He looks like a cartoon version of a goddamn wino.

He comes stumbling over.

"Ty, Jesus, I'm sorry. You know what happened? Here's what happened. I was having lunch with Lou. You remember Lou? I dunno if you ever knew Lou. Anyway, I was having lunch with him about some business — me and Lou are in on this thing, I'll tell you all about it, it's this place these guys are opening, this distillery, me and Lou are gonna invest, it's gonna be big, Ty, I'm telling you, these guys know what they're doing — and then he said, 'They said we should come over and check out a sample batch.' And I was like... well you know me and samples, right? Ha! So I said, 'OK, but I can't stay all night because I'm meeting my son!' But then we got there and Ty, when I tell you that they had ALL the different kinds of whiskey... Man! These guys, they're from Kentucky, I think. Kentucky? Tennessee? Ahhh, I dunno. But they know what they're doing, that's for sure! And they were having this tasting for us because me and Lou, we're thinking about investing because these guys, these Kentucky guys, or Tennessee, they know what they're doing, Ty! Anyway, it put me just a few minutes behind and that's why I'm running late, because, y'know, business, but so I'm sorry I'm late, but I'm here! Let's sit down, eat, eat, c'mon, I'm buying, and... Is that Maddie? Maddie, hey!"

I don't know if it's because it's what Dr. Eldridge put in my head or if it's just because it's what happens. But I do leave my body. I sail right outside of myself and rise above the room and look down on it with my little pad and pen, and what I see is... fucking absurd.

There aren't a ton of other people in Frank's, but there's a few. And they're all looking at us. Victoria has stopped just at the break in the counter and holds the check, unsure whether or not she should make her way over to us. Jack's still stumbling in our direction. It's only a few feet for him to travel, but the whole thing is happening in slow motion. Maddie's got one knee on the booth bench, one foot on the floor, and her grip around my hand is tightening.

And I am dead inside.

The look I see on my face from my reporter's eye-in-the-sky perspective is a completely blank one. It's not disappointment. Or embarrassment. Or sorrow, or shame, or anger. It's simply one of "well, what did you expect?"

"Tyler?" That's Maddie.

"It's OK," I say, squeezing her hand and then letting go to approach him before he can reach me.

"Ty?" she says again as I move toward him. Jack Morgan. My fuckin' dad.

I get to him and he tries to push past me, "No, no, let's sit down. Is that your booth? That's where you're sitting? Did you eat? Lemme buy you something." But I don't let him pass. I put my hands on his shoulders and hold him in place.

"Jack, c'mon. Let's go. Outside. C'mon."

"Noooo. What? Why? Ty, I'm sorry I'm late. I am, but—"

"Jack," I whisper to him. "Outside. Now."

He looks up into my eyes and can clearly see that I'm not fucking around, because he just says, "Yeah... Yeah, OK."

"And pull your fuckin' fly up," I whisper once more.

"Wha—? Oh, shit." He looks down and zips up his pants as I turn him around and send him out the door into the parking lot.

"I'm sorry," I say to Victoria as Jack makes his way out. "Lemme, uh—" I reach my hand out to grab for the check.

"Nah, it's OK," she says, and waves her hand at me not to worry about it.

"No," I say. "No, it's not at all. But one thing's got nothing to do with the other. Please..." Again, I reach my hand out.

Maddie steps over now with a look in her eyes that I have seen before. Not necessarily from her, but from people. It's the look that lets you know that they think they're about to witness something gruesome. Say... someone having the shit kicked out of them, for example.

The one other time I remember seeing it distinctly from Maddie was the night I held a gun to Logan's head in the alley behind Pete's. She didn't know me then. Didn't know a thing about me other than I was the kind of person who probably wasn't afraid to die right then and there.

And it makes me really sad to see that look from her again now.

"Go on," Victoria says again. "It's fine. I've got a dad too."

It's incredible, given the right circumstances, what you can know about a person in five words.

Reaching into my pocket, I pull out a wad of twenties and hand them to her. "Please, just take this."

"I can't."

"Yeah, you totally can. Please."

Maddie reaches over and takes the money from me. She places it in Victoria's resisting hand.

"That was the best milkshake I've ever had," says Maddie, "thanks."

I nod to Victoria and hold the door open for Maddie, who passes me, out into the parking lot. When I turn to follow, I see Jack leaned over the backside of the Tesla having just finished throwing up. Classic. He's now the second member of the Morgan family to throw up at Frank's. Maddie turns to say something to me, but I just walk past her and reach where my father is wrapping up dry-heaving.

I clench my fists, involuntarily, and ask, "How'd you get here?" He points at a pretty new-looking Cadillac sedan parked diagonally across three spaces. Jesus Christ.

"Lou let me take his car," he says.

"You don't have a car?"

He shakes his head. "Been meaning to get a new one, but shit's come up."

"Yeah. OK. I'll call you one."

"No, no, come on! We're gonna hang out, I thought."

"Yeah. We were." I pull out my phone, open the app, and punch in our location. "It'll be here in five minutes," I say.

He nods, absently. "This your car?" he asks, referring to the Tesla.

"No."

"Oh. Thought it must be yours since I heard you got all that money now."

Ladies and gentlemen, more breaking news: Here at Frank's the situation has gotten even more dramatic. Revelations are coming out by the second.

"What? What do you mean?" I ask. "Where'd you hear that?"

"After Thanksgiving," he says, still leaning over, breathing heavy. "I talked to Jenny from the front desk at the Four Seasons. We were just talking and I don't remember how it came up, but she said, 'Your kid is called Tyler?' And I was like, 'Yeah,' and she was like, 'Same last name?' And I was like, 'Yeah,' and she said, 'Tall? Big beard?' And I was like, 'Yeah.' She said you came in personally and reserved the Presidential Suite for five nights over the holidays and I was like, 'Nah, can't be, not the same guy,' but then I, y'know, I used Google and everything and I found out that you invented this like... thing. It said that you were a millionaire! My kid! A millionaire! And I was like, wow! So that's why I wondered if this was your car..."

In the eyes of this investigative journalist, lots of new details are now coming to light.

I take a breath, letting all this absorb its way in and then say, "Shit. *That's* why you came looking for me."

"What?" He coughs.

"That's why you came looking for me. With Evan. You want money."

"What? No!" I don't say anything. And then he goes, "Well, I mean, y'know, I wanted to *talk* to ya about this opportunity. These guys from Kentucky—"

"Or Tennessee, yeah, I got it."

Maddie's looking at me with an expression that's like, *Do you want me to do anything?* I put up my hand and shake my head. She's already doing everything she can do. She's here. Which is all I need from her right now.

And yet again, I pull back up to that birds-eye view of the situation and I see something that now shocks the hell out of me: I'm calm. I don't want to fight anybody or tear anything apart. I don't want to blow this whole place up or torch the earth. I don't feel anger or rage. If I feel anything it's... sorry for him.

Huh. Ain't that something?

And maybe that's what this was supposed to be. Dr. Eldridge asked why I wanted to see him, and I didn't really know. I claimed curiosity, and sure, that's true. But I think I thought I was curious if he and I could resolve something. Or curious to see if maybe he'd changed. Maybe I could get from him something that I missed. Or wanted.

But maybe what I was actually curious about was to see if I could forgive him. Regardless of what he did or didn't do. Regardless of how he's different. Or not.

Maybe that's what I needed from this. Maybe it wasn't for him to give me anything, or for me to get a reclamation of some long-gone, never-to-return father/son what-the-fuck-ever. Maybe it was only ever supposed to be a chance for me to see myself now. And to give myself permission to be at peace with it all. And maybe the fact that I was able to step away from it and see the whole picture instead of just my part of it and my feelings about it is what's allowing that to happen right now.

Wow. Dr. Eldridge is a *really* fucking good doctor.

The car pulls up and I wave the guy over. "Hey, man," I say to the driver, "this is my dad. He's kinda fucked up. So just make sure he gets home, OK?"

The guy eyeballs Jack. "He ain't gonna throw up in my ride, is he?"

"I dunno. Maybe. Look, here's..." I pull out all the cash I have left. "Here's like a couple hundred bucks. If he does, the detailing's on me. If he doesn't, have a happy new year. OK? Cool?"

The driver eyes me for a second, then takes the cash and says, "Yeah. Cool."

Maddie comes over and helps me scoop my dad up and load him into the back seat of the guy's car. As we're plopping him down, he grabs my shirt. "Tyler?"

"Yeah?"

"I'm sorry. I wanted to see you, and... I'm sorry."

The reporter is poised, leaning in, pencil pressed against paper, ready to take note of whatever smartass thing I'm about to say.

"I know, man," I tell Jack. "I know. It's cool. OK? Don't worry about it." And with that, I pat his shoulder, slam the door shut, and the car takes off.

Maddie stands next to me, watching it drive off into the distance. She strokes my arm. "Fuck," she says.

"Yeah," I let out. Then I say, "Well... Look at it this way. At least he recognized me."

She looks over, furrows her brow, then laughs. "You OK?"

"Yeah, I'm OK. Come on. Let's go."

"Where?"

"Back to Evan's. I wasn't kidding, babe. You need to work off those fries." I wink and pat her on the stomach. She slaps my hand away, laughing still.

"Fuck you!"

"That is the plan," I say.

She gives me a kiss and then rounds the car to the passenger side, careful not to step in Jack Morgan's puke. I open my door and plop down. I glance at myself in the rearview mirror. There's a look in my eyes I don't recognize. But I like it. I don't know what it is. But I like it.

Sitting down next to me, Maddie says, "Ask you something?"

"Of course."

"Will you try to see him again?"

I take a second to consider the question. Then... "I dunno. I have no idea. Probably not. I mean if he comes looking for me again, maybe, but... Nah. I probably won't try to find him. I kind of got what I need, I think."

She looks surprised. "Really?"

"Yeah, really."

"OK." After a second, she asks, "How do you feel about it?"

"Which part?"

"I mean are you sad? Relieved? Still hungry? What?" She kind of smiles.

How do I feel? How do I feel? I really have no idea. I never thought I would see him again in the first place. And I suppose that if you had asked me to describe what seeing him again would look like, I would have likely described something not too far off from the way it went. The only thing I wouldn't have described is how I reacted. Helping him into a car. Telling him not to worry.

Being kind about it.

Yeah, that's maybe the only part that surprises me.

So, I look at her with what I think is probably sort of a silly smirk and say, "I dunno. I guess – in the words of the late, great, Walter Cronkite – I just kind of feel like..." I pause to put on a pretty awful Walter Cronkite impression that kind of sounds a lot like my awful Rhett Butler impression.

"That's the way it is."

CHAPTER EIGHTEEN

MADDIE & TYLER

MADDIE

Walking into Evan and Robert's, Tyler heads straight for the windowed doors that open out to the pool. He slides them all the way apart, walks outside where he's being simultaneously illuminated and cast in shadow by the beautiful landscape lights that pop on when it turns dark, and starts taking off his clothes.

"What are you doing?" I ask him.

He doesn't answer, just kicks off his shoes, strips off his t-shirt, pulls off his pants, and stands there, naked, staring at me. The light and steam wafting off the heated pool encircle him and make him look sort of like a ghost. Some kind of lost spirit.

"What are you doing?" I repeat.

And then he jumps in the water. He drops down and then pops back up again, pushing his wet hair back and floating there, still looking at me. I smile because with his bare face and his damp hair, he looks like I remember him from a time many years ago. I think it was maybe a year or so before his mom died. It was summer. Barbara was about to start undergoing intense therapy for her cancer and my parents suggested that we all go out as a group one last time before they knew we probably wouldn't be able to anymore.

They put it to the boys, Scotty, Evan, and Tyler, what they would want to do. All three of them agreed on a water park, so even though I don't think any of the grownups thought that would be the most fun, they went along with it anyway.

I also remember Jack on that day. I mean, I must've been about seven, so I don't think I could have put all the pieces together, but now, looking back... I have a vague recollection of thinking that he seemed different. He had always been a fairly gregarious guy. Not quite as fun or funny as Tyler's mom – because no one was – but still, an OK guy to be around. But that day at the water park, I recall him being sullen. Withdrawn.

Every time I looked over at the grownups I'd see Mom and Dad, Evan's parents, and Barbara all sitting and talking, but Jack would be off to the side with a grownup drink, just sitting by himself. I may just be making this up now – memory is a tricky thing – but I may have marched my little seven-year-old ass over to him and asked if he would want to go on a log flume or some shit. Because, I dunno, seeing people sad and alone used to really bum me out.

And he just kind of waved me off. Ignored me. And then he wandered back over to the bar. I think I shrugged and turned around to see what the boys were doing and that's when I spotted Tyler popping out of the water, laughing and pushing his wet hair out of his face. Looking just the way he does now. And, again, in my memory, that was the moment my tiny little heart fell in love.

Or that could all be bullshit. Like I say... memory. But it feels real to me. Like it tells a story that makes sense. And honestly, if it feels real, then who's to say it isn't?

What I know for sure is that watching Tyler now, treading water and staring at me, my heart is full. I *am* in love. Still and again. And the guy I love is turning out to be the most surprising and at the same time exactly expected version of the guy I wanted him to be. And I can't believe that this is my life. Because not so very long ago, it seemed pretty goddamned impossible to imagine.

I kick off my own shoes now, strip off my top, my jeans and my underwear, and stand there facing him. He doesn't say anything, just continues treading water and staring at me. I walk to stand in the crossover to the outside, letting the tiny chill that's now in the air tickle my skin and make me shiver. I walk over to the edge of the pool by where Tyler is floating and look down at him.

He swims to where I am, props his elbows by my feet and starts stroking my calves with his fingertips. The touch of his hands and the tiny drops of water from his fingers sliding down the backs of my legs causes my shoulder blades to tense up. In a fantastic way. I shudder a little bit and he leans down and kisses the tops of my feet. Then he stretches his neck and licks at my ankle. I close my eyes and throw my head back, letting out the tiniest of groans.

I kneel down, squatting into a sit, and plop myself on the concrete, sliding my legs forward and letting them dangle in the water. Tyler's face is between my knees now and he stares up at me. He still hasn't said a word since we walked in the house. He hasn't had to. He runs his fingers up and down along my thighs as I hold his face in my hands and we look at each other.

His expression doesn't change, and I'm pretty sure mine doesn't either, but we are communicating crystal-clearly. I smile a small, diminutive smile. I hope it's not a sad smile, but I'm sure there's probably some of that in there. Not because I'm actually sad, but because my heart aches for this good, good man who's trying to become an even better man, and with whom I am realizing that I can finally summit that damn mountain. All I needed was to be willing to accept a little help. A climbing buddy. Not because I couldn't do it on my own, but because what the hell would it have even mattered if I had made it to the top alone?

Like I told him in the parking lot of Frank's... *I go where you go.*

And looking in his eyes now, I see where he wants to take us in this moment, and, yeah, it's definitely *way* better than going it alone.

TYLER

I hadn't planned on getting naked and jumping in the pool. I don't know what happened exactly. I've kind of been on autopilot since leaving the diner. I just know that when I walked in the house I had the sudden urge to throw myself into the briny deep. And since we're in the desert and ain't no briny deep to be found, I figured a heated, Olympic-size, salt water pool would do the trick just fine.

I'm sure if I were smarter or more self-aware, I'd be able to unearth the hidden psychological bullshit that would compel me to do such a thing, but I don't really care. All I know is that I needed to feel naked and wet. And now I am.

Looking up at Maddie staring down at me, I detect a tiny bit of sadness in her smile. I don't bother to ask if she's OK. I know the look. It's the look of somebody with a huge heart who hates to see somebody they care about in pain. Which is a look I haven't seen in a long, long time. Maybe from Evan on occasion, but this is different. Obvs.

I don't bother to tell her that I'm not actually in *pain*. It's something else. Ironically, for a long time I was in pain, but didn't show it. What was actually pain got masked by shit that made it look different. On my best days it was just, like, ennui or lethargy or whatever. Just a listless kind of boredom that projected to the world that I didn't care. Most of the time, it was just me looking like an asshole. But I never let the actual pain show through. Anger's funny that way. It's almost never a sincere emotion. It's usually a secondary emotion. A defense mechanism that kicks in to cover fear, or sorrow, or pain, or anxiety. In my case, all of the above.

But now, whatever Maddie's sensing in me isn't any of those things. It's whatever one feels when they've finished running a marathon. Backwards. On crutches. Fighting off a fucking zombie onslaught along the way. And then managed to cross the finish line but with the uneasy suspicion that as soon as they turn around, someone's gonna say, "OK! Ready for the next race?"

But that's life, ain't it? There is no "there" there. And when all is said and done, isn't that actually a good thing? How fucking boring would shit be if you had everything all figured out? I mean, hell, I dunno. As noted, I'm no philosopher. I'm just a naked dude in a pool with the sexiest, kindest, coolest woman I could ever hope to know sitting in front of me with her pussy inches from my tongue.

Yeah. I'm not in pain at all. I'm good.

Gesturing to her with two fingers, I signal her toward me. She wriggles herself forward until her ass is right on the curved edge of the pool before it drops into the water. Just exactly where I can put my face into her perfect softness. Pulling myself up along the wall, I slide forward and run my nose up along the crease between her legs. I nuzzle there, letting my lips and chin tickle at the tender skin. She moans out her agreement and I bring my hands up onto the inside of her thighs to spread her a little wider.

My thumbs find their way to her folds and I separate her opening so that I can embed my nose all the way inside her, drinking in her scent deeply before I tilt my head and allow my tongue to make its way inside next.

Her legs start kicking a little bit in the water behind me, and the soft splashing creates a rhythmic melody that lets me know what I'm doing is pleasing her. Slowly, probably unconsciously, she begins pushing her hips forward, driving herself deeper into my mouth. Which I love, but which is forcing me backwards. We're near the deep end, so I now find myself having to tread water pretty forcefully while at the same time holding her legs just above my shoulders to keep from getting pushed underneath. This is a serious workout and I can feel it in my rib, which... I'm beginning to wonder if it's ever going to heal.

She is now stretched out with her arms straight back and her hands gripping the coping, and I am straining to keep us both aloft. As my tongue does a quick, skittering tap dance across her clit, she arches at the waist, and when she crashes back down, she forces me under the water. I still have hold of her thighs, so I drag her down with me, pulling her off the ledge and underneath we both go.

The lights coming off the inside provide just enough visibility so that I can see the hilariously shocked look on her face. Her hand shoots up to her mouth in surprise and she starts laughing, little air bubbles punctuating her hiccupping glee. The smile that spreads across my face causes tiny bubbles to rise as well, and we grab each other tightly, pulling ourselves together. The kiss we share is longer and harder than it should conceivably be. But we are air, each for the other, like two living SCUBA masks. We breathe life into our shared beings.

Finally, we unlock our embrace and float above the surface, popping out, panting, smiling, shaking our heads because we can't believe... Well, I don't wanna speak for her, but I can't believe that this is my life. Because not so very long ago, it seemed pretty goddamn impossible to imagine. I don't know what she feels, but I'd like to think it's something similar.

We rotate around now, and swim together the few feet back over to the edge of the pool where I prop myself up and she presses her legs against the wall on either side of me. I let my torso float up to meet her, and then she positions herself so that my cock can slide inside her. Gripping me around the waist, she pulls me up and into her over and over again, the water lapping and slapping against us as we make love.

It feels frantic and urgent and necessary, but somehow, at the same time, something about being here in the water slows time down and draws out each moment. Or maybe it has nothing to do with the water. Maybe it's just the way it feels when I'm with her.

Whatever it is, we stay locked together like this for what seems like hours. Back and forth. In and out. Tiny waves rippling along around us. A tidal force generated by the motion of our lovemaking.

We continue not to speak. Neither of us make much of a sound. We only stare into each other, holding tightly and trying not to let go.

And we won't. I know this. I know this is true as much as I have ever known anything. Probably more. We will hold each other forever and then some.

We don't have to say it. We don't have to say a word. It simply is.

I love her.

She loves me.

And we will hold each other.

Now and always.

We will never let go.

"Where are you going?!" I ask, grabbing at her arm to keep her from getting out of the water.

"I have to pee."

"No, don't go. Just pee in the pool."

"I'm not peeing in the pool."

"Why? We just had sex in the pool for like two hours."

"The fact that you see those two things as being somehow similar concerns me."

"OK, fine." I sulk, like the suddenly needy wheeze-box I have just become. "Go pee in the stupid bathroom like a decent, civilized human being. Whatever."

She drops back down in the water and straddles me. "What? What's wrong? Why is baby grumpy?" she asks in what can only be called a "patronizing and yet totally fucking sexy" way.

"I just want to keep you close," I tell her.

"That's sweet."

"Yeah? You don't think I'm a whiny bitch?"

"Sure, I do. But you're a sweet whiny bitch."

I roll my eyes and lift her off me. "Go pee, jackass." She laughs and pulls herself out of the pool. I slap her on the ass as she goes. Water ricochets off her skin into the night air as my hand makes contact, and she squeals.

Once she's gone, out of sight, I allow my head to lean back onto the coping, and, looking up at the stars in the sky, I let out a massive, massive sigh. It's longer and from deeper in my lungs than I think I've ever sighed before. Because it's filled with years of release. A lifetime.

I know that I cannot, in one long breath, let go of everything. I know that I can't breathe out all the hurt, and guilt, and loss, and suffering on just one exhalation. I know that it will take hundreds, probably thousands more sighs to purge myself completely of the weight of friends lost and promises not kept. Of dreams unrealized and goals unfulfilled. I know that there will be demons still lingering in the shadows, and that there will remain mountains to climb and dragons to slay. But I'm good with that.

Because I'm not alone. Because the only person I have ever met in my life who stands a shot of understanding is with me. I told her back on Thanksgiving, when we were having sex in the Four Seasons, that I just wanted her to understand. She said that she wanted that too. And holy shit... she does. I didn't think it was possible for anyone to, but she does.

Looking up at the night sky, I think about how lucky I am. And I laugh. Not because I am lucky, but because I can allow myself to recognize it. To *feel* it. That's something I thought was gone forever. That feeling. That appreciation. That gratitude. And yet here it is. Filling me up and making me smile.

Ain't that some shit?

New Year's Eve is tomorrow. And then a whole new book starts getting written for us. I can't wait to see what happens. Which is fucking incredible since for so long I just dreaded to see what was gonna happen. Man...

Nadir's watch will be ready in a couple of days. Restored. Fixed. And when we find his family and return it, we will be able to know that with every second that it ticks off, it will mark a special, precious, bonus moment in time that Maddie and I will get to share. Moments that didn't have to happen. Moments that all came so very close to never having the chance to be.

I look up into the inky mystery above my head and whisper out, "Thanks."

We really should do something to mark the occasion, I suddenly think. Like, I dunno, maybe we should even get out of town. I know we're gonna be going to the Middle East soon, but that's less of a "vacation" and more of a "Tyler-and-Maddie-continue-to-put-their-lives-at-risk" kind of a getaway. So before that, maybe just something off the grid in a sweet, not war-zoney place. Just for a second.

It's last-minute, but I could get us a flight to somewhere. Find some little B&B on a beach somewhere. Or maybe not a beach. We were just on a beach last week and I dunno if we're far enough removed from that to really enjoy it. Might have Carlos and Logan flashbacks and shit.

Blech.

So maybe one of those treehouse hotels in the jungle. Yeah! That could be rad. Me Tarzan, you Jane and all that. Just running around in loincloths, and eating bananas, and petting monkeys and so forth. Yeah. Yeah, that could be fun. Just a total, wacky, silly change of pace from all that we've been dealing with. Shit, I'm gonna do it right now. Before she gets back from the bathroom. I'll book something on my phone and surprise her. Just tell her to pack a loincloth and give no other hints about what we're doing. That's super-romantic. I'm fuckin' great at this boyfriend shit. I—

"Did you get my texts?"

Because I'm reaching over for my discarded jeans that have my phone in the pocket, I don't see anyone approaching from the indoor portion of the indoor/outdoor space. So that's on me. But, in fairness, I wasn't really expecting someone to show up so rudely, uninvited. Although, if I *had* to pick someone to expect it of... It would be him.

I stop reaching for my phone now, turn to face him, and say, as casually as I can...

"Hey, Logan."

MADDIE

The toilets at Robert and Evan's all have remote controls. It was very jarring the first time I attempted to use one. I was curious what all the little icons on the keypad did. A lot, as it turns out. One of them controls the electronic bidet wand that shoots water up your ass. And everywhere else. And once I figured out that you can control the temperature of the water that sprays up there... Well, now Evan and Robert's bathrooms have become some of my happy places.

And as I'm washing my hands now, I look at myself in the mirror. There's something in my eyes I don't necessarily recognize. But I like it. I don't know what it is. But I like it. It might be contentment. Which is almost as good as a Japanese toilet bidet wand.

Don't get too comfortable, bitch.

Who the fuck was that?

It's me.

Oh, fuck. It's the devil. What the hell is he doing here now?

Whattayou want? I ask.

Nothing. Just to remind you that this ain't your real fuckin' life.

What? What do you mean?

All this shit? All this "comfort" and "generosity" and "nobility" and... "Love..." This ain't you.

Why? Why not? Why the hell not? Why isn't it me?

Because... That shit is for other people. People who can handle it.

What do you mean, "who can handle it?"

Mo' money, mo' problems, sweet cheeks. Mo' responsibility, mo' challenges. Mo' happiness, way, way, way mo' disappointment. And sadness. And pain. You think you can take it? You think you've got what it takes to handle the shit the world throws at you? Really? Like, really, really?

Yeah. I do. I think there's plenty of evidence of that.

The devil cackles.

Oh, shit! That's a good one! Ha! You think you've suffered and now you get to rest? Shit, chick. You have no idea what actual suffering looks like. No idea at all. Sorry, "Angel in Disguise." He says it mockingly. Then adds, *Hashtag RealTalk.*

Fuck this.

Why are you doing this? Where is the angel?

Angel can't help you tonight, pumpkin. Ain't no shelter for you here.

What. The fuck. Are you talking about?

And that's when I hear what sounds like a gunshot.

TYLER

I display as little surprise at seeing him as I possibly can. Which actually isn't that hard because hell, nothing fucking surprises me anymore. So I don't even bother to ask how he survived the fire, or how he found us, or how he got my number to text me, or any of that crap. Because, honestly? Shit don't matter.

No, no, no. Instead of peppering him with dumb questions that won't mean anything five minutes from now, I simply choose to say, "So funny. I was just thinking about you."

"Yeah? What were you thinking?"

Man. He's fucked up. Bad. It's hard to tell just how bruised and battered his face is now, as compared to how it was, because it's currently wrapped in a shitload of gauze. He's limping as he approaches me, gun out, and it's obvious it hurts him to walk. On the plus side for him, he's wearing this, like, burgundy velour tracksuit, so at least he doesn't have to worry about matching his belt to his shoes.

"Oh, y'know," I start, wiping the water droplets off my face, "just about what a crappy time we had at your resort. You should give your cabaña boys towels instead of guns. Just a thought."

I'm working very hard to stay calm even as my eyes dart around behind him to see if I can spy Maddie. If he's done something to her, then it doesn't really much matter what happens to me and I'm just gonna charge this asshole now. If she's OK, then I have to be more tactical about how I handle things to make sure that she stays that way. Either way, things right now are far from ideal. Fuck.

"The wine at the hotel. That was you?" I ask.

He shrugs. Well, at least now I don't feel so silly at being paranoid about not drinking it.

"Get out of the fuckin' pool," he says, gesturing with his pistol.

It's weird. It's weird for him to command me out of the water. As opposed to just shooting me in the fucking head, I mean. I should be used to the notion that dude is terrible at killing people by now – or at least at killing me – but I can't help but wonder what it is he hopes to gain. I can only assume that it's, I dunno, ego. Or something. Maybe dude thinks that because I'm naked in a pool I'm vulnerable? Maybe he thinks that he'll shame me or some shit? Or hell, maybe he just wants to shoot me in the dick. That'd be so fucking lame. Which is so fucking Logan. So I can't put it past him.

"Yeah, OK," I say, and push up on the edge of the wall.

I lift myself out of the pool slowly. Carefully. Keeping my eye on the gun the whole time. I'm not so arrogant to believe that I have anything even close to resembling an advantage right now, but, as with the very first time we met, Logan's first instinct here is not to kill me. It's to threaten me. To intimidate. And even though the odds definitely ain't in my favor, it might just be enough.

Rising out of the water, move by careful move, I feel the night air on my skin. Against the pellets of moisture on my body, it causes my muscles to tense, and flex, and tighten. Which is fine by me because it makes me feel coiled. Ready for whatever is coming next.

As I turn to face him fully, the chill stiffens my neck and I twist it side to side, causing it to crack. Then I take a breath and level off my gaze to look him in the eye. His face is so covered with gauze that the white stands in stark contrast with his brown eyes, making it hard for him to mask where his glance is directed. And there's a flash of a second where I detect something in his glare that I'm choosing to interpret as awe when he eyeballs my cock. It might also just be envy, though. Tough to call.

I suck at my teeth and say, "You're a day early. New Year's Eve is tomorrow."

"Yeah, well," he says, "turns out I'm leaving earlier than I thought."

"Oh, yeah? Where you going? Someplace fun? I hope someplace with a good healthcare system, because it looks like whoever performed your nose job seriously overdid it, bro."

He doesn't say anything for a second. Just looks at me like he's trying real, real hard not to pull the trigger. Which, again, is stupid on his part, and keeps giving me hope. Which may be foolish, but as I've said before, I'm a real cock-sucking optimist.

Also, and this is fucking nuts, I kind of feel bad for him. Just like I did the first time I kicked his and Ricky's asses. I suppose it's a weakness of mine, but seeing him all

201

jacked-up-looking, wearing his dopey tracksuit and limping around like he is makes him seem so... I dunno. Like Fredo from *The Godfather*. Just an idiot who wants so much to be taken seriously. I mean, I'll still kill him, but I'm gonna feel bad about it.

"This is gonna be hard for you to believe," he says, "but I'm not here because you were working for the DEA, or because you and your bitch destroyed what represents years, and years, and *years* of hard work." Calling her a bitch is the closest he's come to really pissing me off. If he calls her anything like that again, I *may* just be forced to rip out this motherfucker's spleen. He goes on, "It's personal. I know, I know. That's cliché and maybe stupid. I should be on a plane right this very second, getting the fuck off the continent. I know. But I just can't. I can't go on living in a world that I know you and that cunt whore of yours are living in too."

Yep. That did it. That's gonna cost him his lower intestine.

"Because," he continues, "Carlos was my fucking uncle, and you killed him. He raised me. And you fucking killed him. And for that, you've gotta pay a goddamn price."

I nod for a sec. Then, "So... *were* you adopted then? Because I've been trying to figure out—"

"Shut up! Just shut your fucking mouth."

"Copy," I tell him. And then I do shut up and look at him like, *Well, go on.*

"Come with me. Now," he says.

He waves the gun to indicate that I should go ahead of him inside. Which I don't like. Once you're on the move to a second location, your odds of survival diminish substantially. And also, fuck this guy.

"Why?" I ask. "If you're gonna fucking do something, do it here."

"Oh, I'm gonna fucking do something all right. And you're gonna watch it happen."

And all of a sudden, I don't feel so cocksucking optimistic.

"Fuck does that mean?"

"You'll see. Let's go."

"Fuck you, dude."

And then the quiet of the desert night is splintered by the sound of a gunshot.

MADDIE

I jump, splashing water everywhere as I do. What the fuck was that?

"Tyler?" I shout as I place my hand on the bathroom doorknob and turn. I yank the door—

And I yank the door—

And I yank the door—

Why the fuck can't I open the fucking door?

It pulls back a couple of inches but that's it. I peer through the open crack and it looks like there's... a rope. Or something. Tied around the door handle. When I strain to see, it seems like the other end is tied around the base of this huge, marble credenza thing that sits in the hallway outside. This whole goddamn house is like a Restoration Hardware showroom, but nicer.

What the fuck is going on? Why is there a rope around—? What the fuck is going on?

"Tyler!" I scream.

I can work my hand through the open crack in the door, but to do that I have to pull on the rope, which makes it taut. And making it taut keeps the slipknot that's tied in it too tight to unravel. I push the door closed a bit to see if I can create some slack, but there's not enough to work the knot free.

"Tyler!"

I tried to tell you, the devil says, *but some people don't wanna listen. Good luck, girlie. You're on your own.* And he disappears.

"TYLER!" I scream.

My brain now starts a violent volley with itself between confusion and a terrified suspicion that I know *exactly* what is going on. The feeling of dread I've been having. The feeling of foreboding. It hasn't been unfounded at all. It hasn't been strong enough.

I yank at the door harder, but I can't get it pulled open beyond a sliver. I decide to see if I can squeeze through. Or, I don't actually "decide" anything. There's no space in my thoughts for decision making. I'm just reacting.

Pressing on the other side of the door, I try to wedge it open enough that I can slide past. I do all the things you do that don't make any sense but feel like they might help. I hold my breath, I stand on my tip-toes to make myself longer and leaner, I pull my shoulders back to see if I can draw my breasts in and flatten my body out. All stupid. And none work.

And so I just start jerking on the handle. Jerking, and jerking, and jerking. Nothing. Nothing works. I am trapped. Something is going on outside of this room, something horrible—and I am trapped.

And there is nothing worse in the whole world than feeling trapped.

TYLER

So you know the thing about getting shot? It hurts. It, no question, stings a little. But more than that, the shit is just fucking surprising. There really is a moment that transcends fear, or pain, or any of that shit, and it's that moment of "Holy fuck! I just got shot!" In addition to being punched, blown up, stabbed, and one time having a Humvee run over my foot (Stupid. My fault), I have been shot, I think, twice. Once in the shoulder and once in the side. Both totally non-lethal wounds. So, it's not like I'm an expert in being shot or anything, but I'm pretty sure that I'll never get used to it. Probably be kinda fucked up if I did.

The bullet that hits me now – the one from Logan's gun – smashes right into my thigh. The thigh is a real tricky area of the body. There's all kinds of shit in the thigh that, while not necessary to sustain life per se, when violated, can really expedite the ending of a life. My only hope, as my legs give out from under me and I fall to the concrete, is that Unlucky Logan managed to miss any of Unlucky Tyler's major arteries or anything like that. If I've caught a break, it will be that it just hit muscle or whatever and didn't fuck up my femoral artery. When I look down, the blood doesn't *appear* to be spurting out like I've seen it do when that artery is hit, but fuck do I know? I ain't no doctor.

Logan comes over to me where I am now bent down growling and trying to put some pressure on the wound. "You wanna know what it means, pretty boy?" he whispers. "Here's what it means. It means that you're gonna come with me and sit there and watch while I finally, finally get to find out what Maddie's sweet pussy tastes like. You're probably gonna want to do something about it, but that hole in your leg is just the first one you're gonna get. So, while Maddie gets to find out what it feels like to have my tongue inside her and my cock in her ass, she'll also know that you're dying in front of her the whole time. And then after you're good and gone, I'll finish up and send Maddie off to join you. Yeah, I'm gonna let you two burn in Hell together, because that's the kind of generous soul I am. Now let's. Fucking. Go."

He has the gun right at my temple and his mouth is right by my ear.

And being close enough to me that I can get my hands on him is his first mistake.

His second mistake is letting me know that, at least at present, Maddie's OK. I don't know where she is inside, and I don't know if he has hurt her in some way, but based on what he just said, I know that she's at least alive.

And when you put those two mistakes together, you get what happens next.

"Please," I plead. "Please, please, please. Do whatever the fuck you want to me, but just please don't hurt Maddie." I can't imagine he's stupid enough to believe this horseshit, but then again... Yeah. I can.

And when he reaches down to pull me up and drag me with him, I take him by the arm and yank him as hard as I can, smashing his bandaged and fucked-up face into the concrete. He screams. Loud. There's no other houses around, so nobody can hear him scream, nobody can hear the gunshot, and nobody can hear everything that pops off next. Nobody to get in the way and get hurt, but nobody to call for help either.

Which could be a good thing or a bad thing, but right now... it just is.

And all I can think is that it's probably for the best because shit's about to get real, real bloody out here.

And I hope to fucking Christ that Maddie is OK.

Please be OK, Maddie.

Please be OK.

MADDIE

I hear a scream. A loud scream. A scream of pain.

And I lose my shit.

I'm kicking the door, and pulling at the handle, and looking around like maybe there's another way out of here even though I know there isn't. No window, no other exit. This is it. I have to get the fuck out of here. I have to.

Opening the drawers to the vanity, I'm looking for something. Anything. I don't know what. A chainsaw would be helpful, but I'm not seeing one. I kick the door one more time and my foot accidentally hits the handle. And it shakes.

It kind of bounces. Like maybe it can be loosened. Or dislodged. Or knocked the hell off. And if it can, then the rope will fall with it. It's not so much a long shot as it is something that is gonna fucking hurt.

But... I know I can shoulder pain.

So fuck it.

I rear back and kick it again and this time I miss the handle with my heel and the soft, fleshy part of my foot makes full contact.

"Motherfucker!"

I'm limping around in circles, trying to shake it off. It's the kind of jarring, stabbing pain that runs all the way up the leg and feels like it ends in your hair. But oh, well.

I kick at it again, this time landing squarely on the knob with my heel. It is equally as painful, but just in a different way. The pain is also mitigated by the fact that the knob now seems to be jangling loose. It's wobbly. I pull at it to see if I can tug it off.

Not quite. Shit.

I'm going to have to go all in one more time. I'm sure I'm in more pain than I can realize, but right now I'm just grateful that adrenaline works the way it does. I put one hand on the sink basin, one hand on the wall on the other side, glance over at myself in the mirror, and, addressing the devil, say aloud...

"You're wrong, asshole. I'm a bitch who can handle anything."

And then I turn, and with all my might, I level my foot at the knob and that motherfucker snaps right off the stem and goes ricocheting off the wall. I actually have to duck to keep from getting beaned in the head.

I scream out, half in pain, half in victory, and push out the remaining stem that holds the front of the handle with the rope on it. The latch is still in position, but I can slide my finger in the hole where the stem was and draw it back far enough to yank the door open and free myself. I take off down the hall, unconcerned with what's waiting for me outside, and with only one thought in my head...

I hope to fucking Christ that Tyler is OK.

Please be OK, Tyler.

Please be OK.

TYLER

Even though Logan is wailing and moaning, he manages to keep his grip on the gun. I go to wrest it from him, but he manages to kick me off him, nailing me hard right in my still-healing rib.

"Motherfucker!" I let out, as I fall backwards and see the blood pumping harder from the wound in my leg. He's holding his face now, trying to turn and aim at me again. And all I can think is, *You stupid fuck. This is why you don't give someone a second chance.* Oh, well.

I lurch toward him and the searing pain in both my side and leg are making it hard for me to see clearly. Everything's kinda fuzzy and hazy, but I can see shapes, and I charge straight for the douchebag-shaped asshole I can make out in front of me. Hammering towards him in my naked, scarred, and bloody state, I wonder what this would look like if someone did happen upon it. A guy with a mummy face in a burgundy velour tracksuit and a bleeding, naked dude mixing it up poolside in a ridiculous mansion in the desert. They'd probably think, *Look, Gertrude! They're making a movie!* And despite everything, that makes me smile for the tiniest measure of time.

I lunge into Logan to keep him from leveling his weapon at me, and of course...

We both careen backwards into the fucking pool.

The blood from my leg fans out in thin ribbons through the water. And now we're grasping and poking and punching at each other, the weight of our struggle pulling us toward the bottom. We're at the deep end. Deep enough that the surface is just above our heads.

At this point, I'm still more worried about getting the gun out of his hand than I am about drowning or bleeding out or any shit like that. I don't *think* I'm gonna bleed out, and I really don't *think* I'm gonna drown. I was in the fuckin' Navy. And even though most of my work was terrestrial, I had plenty of water training and I know that my lung capacity is solid and more or less how long I can struggle under water before I'll need to take in air. I'm sure I can outlast this cocksucker.

I'm sure I can.

So, at present, my strategy — if you can call it a fucking strategy — is just to keep him pinned down so that the gun isn't pointed my way and so that he can't get out from underneath me until his fucking chest fills with water and he goes to sleep. Then I'll crawl out of here, find Maddie, make sure she's OK, and then get us to a goddamn motherfucking treehouse where nobody can find us! Fuck!

At least, that's my plan until he knees me in the ribs again, and when I yelp, I take in a whole, big-ass mouthful of water and swallow it down. Shit. Well, so much for outlasting him. Fuck me.

OK.

Plan B.

MADDIE

Ow. It fucking hurts to walk. So good thing I'm not walking. I'm in a full sprint, running naked through the house to get to the pool. I tear down the hallway and make it to the indoor portion of the indoor/outdoor space. Looking out onto the deck, I don't see anything right away. No Tyler. No nothing. Which worries me.

And then I see something that worries me more.

There's little slivers of dark color in the water being illuminated by the lights from inside the pool. And the water itself is churning and splashing. Just underneath I can see two bodies. Tyler and someone who I can't make out to determine for certain, but who is one hundred percent undoubtedly Logan.

I just know it.

When I asked Tyler if he was sure that Logan had died in the fire, he assured me that he had to have. And right then and there I knew, I just felt it in my gut, that we would see him again. I didn't say anything because I was hoping against hope that I was just being nervous and shell-shocked. But inside, intuitively... I knew.

The fight I see happening is bizarre. I can't really make everything out. Just enough to see that Tyler is on top and that it looks like... he's winning? Maybe? It's impossible to know. It's also impossible to know where the blood is coming from. Who's bleeding, I mean. But the one thing I do know is that I'm not just going to stand here debating with myself about it.

And as I'm at the edge of the pool, about to jump in... I hear the shot.

TYLER

I struggle with my left hand to pull the gun from his right. But he's fighting me, boy. He's hanging on for dear life, that's for sure. Cockroaches and Logan. Hard to friggin' kill. Son of a bitch.

And now things are starting to get dark. Which I mean literally. My vision is really getting cloudy. I don't know if it's loss of blood, oxygen, or probably a combination of both, but the lights are going out at Casa Tyler. Fuck me. Is this really how I'm going to die? Seriously? Drowning? Not getting shot, or blown up, or burned up, or anything like that, but in almost the exact *opposite* way? Man. Ain't that some shit?

And with the last bit of energy I have left, I open my mouth once more and howl a muted and strangled cry of rage and desperation, taking in what feels like a river of anger into my lungs, and I wrench the gun from Logan's weakening hand, point the barrel towards his chest, and fire.

The muffled cough of the bullet leaving the pistol thuds in the water as the slug pierces Logan's breastplate. It's hard to tell immediately if it did in fact make the contact that I think it did, because the burgundy of the tracksuit masks the emerging stream of blood. But quickly, it becomes clear that it did find its target, because Logan stops fighting and his eyes stay open in an expression of terminal shock.

Sorry, Logan.

No. That's a lie. I'm not sorry. We all make choices in life.

And Logan made his.

And now I see the trickle of blood seeping out from the wet velour, and I realize... he's gone. He's really, really gone. There will be no mistake this time. No uncertainty. No last-minute surprises. He's gone.

Fuck you, Logan. Fuck you straight to hell.

But, as with all things in life, there is a cost for this moment. Nothing, and I mean nothing, happens without sacrifice. And as the darkness now comes over me fully, and I can no longer pretend that I'm going to climb out of here and go with Maddie to a treehouse someplace, I have only two thoughts in my mind.

And if you had asked me to tell you what my final thoughts would be when the time came, there's no way I would've picked these weirdo ones in a million years, but...

I think, one: *Fuck. Now I'll never find out Logan's story. Like was his mother Carlos's sister, or...?*

And two: *Shit. This is way worse than Maddie peeing in the pool.*

MADDIE

The water acts as kind of a silencer, so it's not like the one I heard from the bathroom, but it's loud enough to make me stop me in my tracks for a second. My entire body freezes.

And then the worst thing that can happen does. The thrashing stops. The struggling abates. As activated as the violent frenzy of the fight I was just witnessing made me, the contrasting stillness is numbing. And now the tiny streaks of blood I saw turn into a full, rich pool. A pool inside a pool. A pool I jump into screaming, "NO!" as I leap.

I swim down and wrap my arms around the heavy, scarred, lifeless frame of Tyler Morgan and begin trying to pull him to the surface. It's hard. Because he's big. And dead weight is heavy to lift.

Dead weight.

The words echo inside my head as I struggle and lift, trying to draw him out. I strain, and tug, and as I get to the edge and almost have him up, he slips from my grip and goes floating back down to the bottom. *Shit!* I don't know if I can do it. I'm out of breath, and he's heavy, and if I can't get him up... What do I do then?

I think about how he didn't want me to go to the bathroom before. How he wanted me to stay here with him. And how cute it was, and how we gave each other shit.

And it makes me sad.

I go where you go, Ty. Wherever that takes us.

It runs through my head, over and over and over again.

I go where you go.

And that's the thought that propels me to kick off the wall and swim back down to the bottom. And try again.

Because I don't care what happens to me.

I only care what happens to us.

I go where you go, Tyler Hudson Morgan.

I go where you go.

CHAPTER NINETEEN

TYLER

"Hello, Mr. Morgan. Welcome back."

She's young. Pretty. Dark skin and dark hair. Her eyes are almost as black as Evan's, but not quite. Nobody's are that dark, but hers are close. She wears a flowy, billowy, formless dress. Not diaphanous exactly, but comfortable-looking. The fabric has a complicated floral pattern. Flowers that I'm not sure I've ever seen before.

She goes to put a lei around my neck and that's when I look down and see that I'm not wearing a shirt. Just white linen pants that look kind of like pajama bottoms. Which I have never owned and am not sure how they found their way onto my body.

But that feels secondary. Because what's particularly noteworthy is not that I don't have on a shirt. What's particularly noteworthy is what else seems to be missing.

My scars.

She hands me a fruity-looking drink served in one of those resort-style, hourglass-looking drink glasses. The ones that start out as colored at the bottom and then get clear as they travel up the stem to the main part—the vessel, I guess.

I let her put on the lei and kiss me on both cheeks, then I stand there, holding the glass as the frosty rivulets of condensation slide down the side and over my hand, and I say, "I'm sorry, have I been here before? Where am I?"

She smiles and squints her eyes like she's confused by the question. Then she tilts her head to the side, her smile widens, and she says again, "Welcome back."

She bows slightly. I bow in return, sort of reflexively, and then she glides away.

I place the straw from the drink to my lips and sip, absently, as I look around to take in my surroundings. It's tropical. Jungle-like. But there is also the evidence of a man-made footprint. There are two stone obelisks. Two giant pillars that lift well above where my eye can track, but instinctively, I have the sense that they are holding something up. They're beautiful and ornamental, but simultaneously generate an aura of functionality.

And there's water everywhere. Oceans of it in the distance. Pools of it in the foreground. Droplets of it on my glass. A waterfall behind me. A stream in front of me. And everywhere, lush, rich, textured landscape grows and flourishes freely.

I take another sip of my drink. Partially just because I'm holding it and partially because it's motherfucking delicious. It tastes like all the fruits I like came together into one super-fruit and then instead of the mixture of flavors competing for dominance, they worked out some peace treaty to balance perfectly in what I can only describe as a flavor orgy. It's like my mouth is being fucked blissfully into euphoria.

I gotta get this recipe.

I'm not the only one here. There are dozens of people wandering around. Maybe hundreds. Some look like me, a little dopey and confused, but sipping their drinks with an expression of "holy fuck, that's good," on their faces. Some look amused at the rest of us. Like they've been wherever we are for a while and they already know how fucking good the drinks are.

I don't see Maddie.

Another dark-skinned, dark-haired, dark-eyed beauty walks by me. He wears the same loose-fitting, billowy, not-quite-diaphanous dress thing as the other one. I call to stop him. "Hey, man, 'scuse me." But he just keeps walking.

I trot after him, trying again. "Sir? 'Scuse me." Again, he keeps going. I try one last time, shouting, "Hey, friend?"

And then he turns to see me. "Yes?"

"Sorry. I didn't mean to shout. I didn't know if you could hear me."

"Oh, that's fine. *I'm* sorry. I didn't realize you were talking to me."

"Oh, I—"

A hand rises to cut me off. "Happens all the time."

And then, for some reason I couldn't explain if I had money riding on it, I understand why this beautiful creature didn't stop.

Because they are not him. Or her.

They are not here. And they are not away.

They are everywhere. And they are nowhere.

They are all of us. And they are none of us.

And in their company... I feel safe.

"Cool. Well, still," I offer. "My bad."

"It's all love," they say. And I believe it on about three different levels.

"So, um, do you happen to know where my girlfriend Maddie is?" I ask.

The expression that comes back my way is one I've never seen before, so I can't describe it. It's not one of amusement, or kindness, or wisdom, or comfort, or patience.

It's all of them at once.

"We don't keep inventory. But those over there might be able to help you."

And as I turn to look where they're pointing, I discover that I have sharper reflexes than I ever knew. Because when my jaw goes slack and my grip loosens, allowing the glass to fall from my hand and go careening to the floor, I'm able to snatch it up before it hits the ground.

The group I see is standing knee deep in a wading pool, all gathered around a circular table that comes just below chest height, talking and laughing and sipping their own drinks. My heart starts beating fast. Just like it did when I was in my kitchen on Halloween night and Maddie asked me what my real name was. Unlike then, though, I don't feel like I'm having a heart attack. It actually just feels like my heart is... growing somehow. I don't know if that's even anatomically possible, but it's how it feels. It also feels like it's going to burst through my chest and splatter the surroundings in my fucking arterial spray.

And as quickly as it feels like it started beating, it almost as quickly feels like it stops when the group, as one, looks over at me. They're not laughing, but they are still smiling, and then they peel away from the table, en masse, to approach me.

Which is fine. Because I'm frozen. I can't move. Just like I couldn't move those couple times in Mexico. Just like I froze up then. But this isn't anxiety or some kind of weird flashback. This is just... stillness. A stillness that I want to live in.

The members of the group fall into a single file line. A receiving line. They make their way across the pool to where I'm standing, and for the first time, I realize that I'm also standing about ankle deep in water. It's cooling. Soothing. It definitely feels like water, but it feels like something else too. Something I can't quite identify. If I had to put a word to it, though, I might call it... memory.

The first one to step to me and take my hand is Jeff.

"Hey, man," he says.

"Uh... hey. Dude," I manage to work out.

He takes a sip of his drink, and as he pulls it away from his mouth, he gestures with it to me and asks, "What's yours?"

"Uh... not sure."

"Yeah." He nods. "It's good though, right?" There's a gleam in his eye. That same youthful, excited gleam he had when he told me that we'd be going to a strip club for his birthday. About ten percent more enthusiasm than is probably necessary over something like a fruity drink. Or maybe it's *exactly* the right amount of enthusiasm. Either way, he raises his glass to me in a "cheers" motion, we clink them together, and he pats me on the shoulder and walks off, sipping happily.

I watch him go. I have things I want to ask him, things I want to say, but he disappears before I get a chance.

And then Pete approaches.

"Tyler," he says, in his Pete way. He's still wearing one of his aloha shirts, which looks totally at home in this new environment. "You shaved."

Shaking my head a wee bit, I work out, "Hey, Pete." We shake hands. His grip is stronger than I remembered. Then I ask, "Pete... What—?"

But he stops me. "Don't ask questions you already know the answers to. Makes you sound like an asshole," he says.

Fair enough.

Then he waves to someone to come join him. A woman approaches. A pretty, slightly round, kind-seeming but also no-nonsense-looking woman. Basically, the female version of Pete.

She steps up next to him, extends her hand, and I take it. "You're Tyler?" she asks.

I nod as we shake. "You're Carolina," I offer as fact. She nods in kind.

"Pete tells me you're pretty stupid," she says, not joking.

"Um, yeah. I mean, I have been. Yeah. He ain't wrong."

She nods, thoughtfully. "No wonder you two get along so well." She looks at him and smiles. He smiles back. Then he bends to her and they kiss.

I smile at them both. This is the only time I've ever seen Pete approaching anything that resembles sweet, and so I take the opportunity to ask him, "You, uh... You like me, Pete?"

Pete stops kissing his lady, lets his smile drop, and says, "Drink your fruity-ass drink and shut up, kid." And as they walk off past me, they both stroke my shoulder.

I drop my head as they walk away and let out an enormous sigh. I bend down into a crouch, steeling myself for what's coming next. Leaving my drink in the pool of water, I stand back up again, lift my head, and in the next moment, before any words can even be exchanged, I am lost inside a hug with my old friend.

I clasp my hand around the nape of Nadir's neck and he grips the back of my head. We hold each other like that for what feels like a hundred years. And who knows? Maybe it is.

When I finally pull away from him, I almost start crying. Because he looks like him. Not the way he looked when I last saw him, but the way he looked in the moments just before that. Happy, and grinning, and joyous, and whole.

I take his face in my hands, my own head twisting back and forth, unable to grasp that this is really happening.

"Nadir..." It's all I can say.

"Tyler. Tyler, my friend," he responds.

There's so, so, so much that I don't know how to begin. So I decide to work backwards. "I'm, um... I'm getting your watch fixed."

"It is your watch," he tells me, laughing. "I gave it to you."

"I know, but..." I run out of words. His smile widens.

"It is good to see you," he says.

"Nadir, I'm so sorry. I—"

He puts his finger on my lip and shushes me. "Tyler, shhhh. Being sorry requires sorrow. And there is none of that now."

"But—"

221

"There is no need for explaining. There is no need for regret. Because here..." He gestures all around us. My breath catches in my throat. "Here," he says again, "it is *always* morning."

And I can't hold it anymore. I start to cry. And I begin stammering out, "But I didn't do what I should have. Your family... The work you wanted to do... I didn't..."

"My friend." He takes me by the shoulders, "There is no past, so there is nothing you didn't do. There is only now. And now you are doing exactly what it is that you should. All is as it should be, my dear, sweet Tyler. You are a good man. And that is enough. Please. Know this."

I sniff back a couple of the tears and I hug him again. He hugs me back and laughs.

"There will be much time for us to know each other again. Much time. If you wish it so. Will you stay?"

I pull back out of the hug with him again. This is a question that I didn't even know could be asked.

"Do I have a choice?"

He narrows his eyes in a gentle and thoughtful way and says, "Always." Then he steps back and holds out his hand to the side, readying to slap his palm into mine in the same clasp of solidarity we used when we cemented our partnership all those years ago. I reach back and throw my hand into his, and we shake our unified fist.

"I am glad to see your face," he says. "And whether soon or even sooner than that... I will see it again." And then he releases my grip and begins to head off.

"Wait," I say, stepping in front to stop him. "Where are you going?"

He grins. "I am happy to see you. But it is not me you are here for now."

"What do you mean?"

Still grinning, he says, "I will see you the next time I see you." He puts his hand over his heart and bows to me. "As Salaam Alaykum. My brother."

And then he places his palm on the side of my face, pats me, and as he walks away, I turn to see him follow where the others went. Somewhere off into the sprawling jungle. Behind one of the waterfalls and out of sight.

It's not him I am here for.

I take a massive breath and blow it out. Yep. Yep. I get it. I know.

I know.

And when I turn back around...

"'Sup, T?"

I draw all the strength I have and say...

"Hey, Scotty."

Wow. He's so grown. Strong. So much older than the last time I saw him. He still has the same red hair and freckles that made him look like some nineteen-fifties version of what they used to call an "all-American boy," but it no longer makes him look boyish and cute. Instead, it comes across as rugged and resolved.

I saw pictures of him in those years after I left, but it's not the same as seeing him now. In my memories of him, he's always been little Scotty. The Scotty I knew from childhood. The Scotty I knew from high school. Not the man that Scotty became.

But the man is here now. Standing right the hell in front of me.

He saunters up and lands inches from my face. There's a smirk of knowing confidence in his eyes. He tilts his neck to one side. Then the other. Then he squares off and looks dead into me.

"So," he says. "You're banging my sister?"

"Wha—? Scotty—it's not—"

And then he starts laughing. "I'm fucking with you, bro!" He grabs me and pulls me into a bear hug. My arms dangle at my sides for a moment before I remember to raise them and hug him back.

"Dude," he says, pulling back and grabbing my shoulders. "Look at you. You look so much better without that crazy beard. You never should've let that thing get so out of hand. You won't do that again, right?"

"Probably not, but... Wait. How did you know about my beard?"

"I've been watching you, bud."

"Whatayou—? You have?"

"Yeah. Of course I have. All the time."

The very, very first thought I now have is *Oh, God, does he mean like ALL the time?*

"No, man," he says, before I even have a chance to say anything. Which is weird. "No, I, like, turn the channel when you and Maddie...y'know. I watch hoops or whatever."

"Scotty, I just... I..." And suddenly, I have a terrible feeling. "Is Maddie here *now?*"

"Maddie? Oh, no. No way. No, not her time yet."

"Oh. OK. Good," I say, dropping my head just a bit. Both in relief and in sadness.

"Hey." He bends his head to find my eyes. "Dude, don't be bummed. You don't have to stay if you don't wanna."

That's what Nadir said too. What does that mean?

"It means..." he starts. Which is, again, weird, because I didn't ask the question aloud. "You don't have to ask it aloud," he says.

OK. Fine. I quit.

"It means," he says again, "that you're not done yet either. Not if you don't want to be. It's really no more complicated than that. Up to you."

"Wait. Are you saying that I get to choose when I die?"

"Well, no. Not exactly. I mean at some point it's just gonna happen, but for you, after everything *I've* done to get you and Maddie together? I would consider it a personal favor if you'd go and actually *be* with her."

A cold chill runs through me because this all sounds startlingly familiar to the shit I heard when I died the last time. But there's no danger of Scotty reading my thoughts at this moment, because there are none. Just a baffled, slack-jawed look on my face and an empty space in my skull where my brain used to be. I think. Or don't. Whatever.

"Wait. What do you mean, after what *you* did to get me and Maddie together? I thought..." And then I remember what James Franco told me after the debacle with my apartment fire. He said, "People see me how they wanna."

So I ask the suddenly obvious question. "Scotty? Are you God?"

"Um... Well. Yeah. I am."

I'm glad I'm dead, because otherwise I *would* have a heart attack.

"And so are you," he goes on. "And so is Nadir, and Pete, and Carolina, and Jeff, and those guys over there, and that chick with the hat, and they who welcomed you, and Maddie, and.... All of us, man. We all are."

"What? What are you saying?"

"All of us. All the people and plants and animals and everything. That's what God is, dude. We're all

225

accountable, each to the other. *That's* God. So yeah, I mean... I'm God too."

And I thought my mind was blown the last time.

"So James Franco *isn't* here?"

He draws his chin back into his neck in seeming confusion. "James Franco? Why the fuck would James Franco be here?"

"I—He wouldn't. No reason. *You're* the one responsible for me and Maddie being together?"

"Well, kind of. I mean, you and Maddie are the ones actually responsible, but I did my best to make sure you got there. I mean... I dunno. Call it 'guardian angel,' call it 'mortal protector,' call it 'good friend,' call it whatever you want. I've just been trying to get you and Maddie together for a long time. Ever since I made the choice to cash in my own chips. But you made it really, *really* hard. So, all I'm saying is that now that you've *finally* hooked up, it would mean a lot to me, personally, if you'd just go back and do right by her. That's it."

I take a second. This should be an easy choice. Of course I want to go back and be with Maddie. Of course I do. And yet I have to ask, "What's it like here?"

"What do you mean?"

"I mean, is there really like no suffering and is it morning all the time like Nadir said, or...?"

He shrugs. "Up to you, man. That's all just a reflection of you. But it seems like things must going OK right now because, I mean... You made *this*." He gestures all around him. "Nice work."

"What? I did? How did I?"

"Because *you're God*, man. You can do anything. And you don't have to be here to do it. You can make all of this on earth, if you want. I mean, maybe not the towering obelisks. There are probably building codes and stuff, but you get what I'm saying. There's no point in waiting to find Heaven. It's all already there. You just have to seize it."

I just stare at him now, because what he's saying seems...

Well, it seems...

Obvious.

"'Our deepest fear is not that we are inadequate. Our deepest fear is that we are powerful beyond measure,'" I mumble to myself.

"What? What is that?" he asks. "Oh, is that from that Nelson Mandela speech?"

"Yeah. But it wasn't actually Mandela. It was Marianne Williamson."

"No. Pretty sure it was Mandela."

"Nope. It wasn't. Maddie told me."

"Really?"

"Yeah."

"Huh. I'll have to ask Mandela why people think it was him."

There's a lot that I want to say, so I just launch in. "Scotty, I—"

"Stop," he says, putting up his hand. "You don't have to say it, man. You said everything at my grave. We're good." He takes me around the back of the neck and presses his forehead to mine. "We're good."

I just stand there for a moment, feeling the touch of my long-lost best friend one more time. Something I thought I'd never get again. And then, after an endless-seeming while, I say, "Can I ask you something?"

"Why did I want it to be you with Maddie?"

I nod. Our heads are still touching, so it causes both of our necks to move in unison.

"Because," he says, "there's no one else it could have been." Then he slaps me on the shoulder and says, "Gotta go."

"No. Wait! What? Why? Where are you going?"

"I'm not sure. But I'll find out when I get there. Kind of how it works here."

"I mean I'll go back and all, especially if that's what you want, because, I mean, it's *absolutely* what I want, but... Can't we just hang for a little while?"

His lips press together tightly, and he shakes his head. "Can't, man. Gotta run. Besides, until you get back, I wanna keep eyes on Maddie. Know what I mean? I have a feeling she's freaking out right now. Besides, it's not really me you're here for."

"What? What does that mean?"

"I'll see you again, man. OK? I will. Promise." He smiles, turns, and also heads off in the direction that Jeff, Pete, Carolina, and Nadir went.

And quite suddenly I also now realize that everyone else is gone too. All the other people who were here who looked like me, all the people who were here who looked like them, everyone. I'm just standing alone, ankle-deep in water, looking out over a seemingly endless horizon at the most indescribably placid universe I've ever seen, with somehow quiet waterfalls cascading all around.

And then, out of nowhere, I hear the soft splash of feet moving through the water behind me.

And at the same time, I catch a whiff of cinnamon.

Turning slowly, I can already feel the pressure building behind my eyes. My breathing turns sharp and shallow and I feel like I might hyperventilate. As my shoulder shifts into the direction of the approaching footsteps, I can feel my body starting to vibrate with energy. And when I make it all the way around, I cannot continue standing.

My legs give out from under me slowly, muscle by muscle, like someone shutting off the lights in an office building floor by floor, and I fall to my knees in the pool, my shoulders beginning to shudder and my head to shake. And through the tears streaming down my cheeks like the waterfalls spilling around me, I see her.

Mom.

She's wearing the same clothes she was wearing the day she collapsed in the kitchen. A soft, yellow sweater that beams like the sun and falls off one of her always tan shoulders. A pair of faded jeans that she has rolled up around her calves to keep them from getting them wet. A simple gold chain that I gave her for her birthday the year before. Bought with money that I had been saving for months, any time I could get my hands on some.

Her dark hair hangs down around her neck, and her eyes – my eyes – are as deep and blue as the oceans that surround us. She's so beautiful. And it makes my heart hurt to realize this, because I almost forgot.

She is thirty-eight years old.

She comes to where I am kneeling down and stands over me. My chin is buried in my chest because I'm afraid to look up. I can't stop crying. She rubs my hair, and I cry harder.

"Shhh. Shhh." I hear her voice. Not in my memory, or in my imagining, but here, now, in my actual presence, for the first time in seventeen years. "Tyler... Tyler, honey. Look at me."

She kneels down as well. I see her knees landing in front of mine and resting in the water. She takes my chin in her hands and raises my head upright so that she can see me. She smiles the smile of a mother who hates to see her child in pain but knows that the pain can be cleaned away by a mother's loving touch.

She puts her palms on my tear-drenched cheeks and commences wiping the tears away, which just makes me cry more. I'm sniffling and sobbing, my shoulders heaving up and down, and she just keeps wiping my face and whispering, "Shhh. Shhh."

After some moments of this, my tears begin to slow, and my breathing starts to level out. She's still wiping my face and rubbing her hands across the front of my hair. The smile is still there, and when I reach up to place my hands over hers, I jolt at the sensation of touching her, and she laughs.

"Hey, buddy," she says.

It's weird to question something appearing as true, but humans do it all the time. We say, "Really?" Or, "No way!" Or, "Are you serious?" Almost as a reflex. It usually doesn't mean that we don't believe. It more means that we want to express astonishment. But right now, in this moment, when I say, "Mom?" It's a real goddamn question.

"Yep," she says with a shrug in her voice. "It's me. Hi."

I reach out and touch her face, carefully. I let my fingertips trace the contours of her cheeks and the shape of her nose. I let them spread across her forehead and gently close her eyelids. They land on her lips and her chin. And then...

She goes, "Boo!"

And I stumble backwards and land on my ass in the water.

She starts laughing, hard, and rushes over to me. "I'm sorry, I'm sorry, baby," she says, still laughing, "I know I shouldn't, but I couldn't resist."

Yep. That's my mom.

She helps me up to my feet, and we stand there just staring at each other. I forgot how tall she is. She's the one I get my height from. But the last time I saw her, I only came up to about her chest. Now, I'm a good four or five inches above her.

"You got so big," she says.

"Yeah," I say. "Yeah. That happens."

She smiles and says, "I guess it does."

"I can't believe you're here," I say.

"Why?" she asks.

"Because... Because I never thought I'd see you again."

"Well, baby," she says, reaching for my hands, "it's what's happening right now, so you may as well choose to believe it." And she winks.

I look down at our interlocked fingers. "I've missed you," I sigh out.

"Really?" she says. "Because it doesn't feel like you've missed me at all."

I snap my head up, mortified. "What? Why? Why do you say that?"

"Because you think about me all the time. I feel it. I'm always there. I haven't gone anywhere."

"But... But that's not what I mean. I—"

She presses our hands together and says, "I know what you *mean*. I'm just talking about what *is*." And she

231

looks at me with her head tilted in a total Barbara Hudson Morgan way. "You get what I'm saying, right?"

I let out a breath and nod. "Yeah. I do."

"I know you do. You're smarter than you like to let on." She smirks again, and I laugh.

"Am I?"

"You know you are. But I'm proud of you that you don't go around showing off about it. You've got so many other gifts that if people knew you were smarter than them too, they'd *really* be annoyed with you."

"You mean as opposed to the just regular level of annoyance I inspire now?"

"Exactly," she says. And we both laugh.

When the laughter dies down, the gentle lapping of water all around us is all I can hear.

"It's beautiful here," I say.

She nods and looks around. "Yeah. You did a good job."

"Is this really all me?"

"Yep," she says, "it sure is." Then, after a moment of continuing to listen to the water, "How's Maddie?"

I can't stop the smile from spreading. "She's good," I say over my dippy grin.

"Yeah?" she says, grinning too. "You love her, huh?"

"Like, more than I thought it was possible to ever love anything or anyone. Which is to say, at all. But, like, way more even than *that*."

She chuckles. "Good."

After another beat, I ask, "Mom?"

And instead of saying, "What?" she answers the question still in my head. "Because I felt about him the way you feel about Maddie, baby."

"You did? Really? How?"

"Because. He wasn't always the way he is. You remember." The look on her face is a sad one, which makes me sad.

"Yeah. Yeah. I do." This is painful and feels like it's ruining the moment. I wish I hadn't brought it up.

"No. It's OK for you to wonder about it," she says. "I'd be concerned if you didn't."

I nod and let out a huff or air.

"Hey," she says. "Think about this: I loved your father more than anything or anyone. And he felt the same way about me. Honestly, babe, we were just like you and Maddie. Well... not *just* like. You guys have one hell of a story to tell your kids one day." She winks. "But we felt exactly as strongly as you do. Now think about something happening to Maddie."

"Mom..."

"I know, it's gross, but do it." She's right. It is gross. But I do. "Now imagine what *that* would feel like."

I take this in.

I get it. I get what she's saying. If anything happened to Maddie now and she was taken from me, there's no telling what I might do. Woe be to the earth, because Tyler Hudson Morgan would...

Wait. No. He wouldn't. I mean, no, I wouldn't. I wouldn't go on some rampage and just hurt myself and the world. Not anymore. Not again. Because that's not what Maddie would want. That wouldn't be kind. That wouldn't be honoring her. That wouldn't be honoring myself. I wouldn't...

Her smile widens, and she says, "And that's why you're my favorite son."

"But wait," I say. "But Dad..."

"He doesn't have the advantages you do, honey. Not here"—she points at my head—"and not here." And she points at my heart. "You're way ahead of him. And what you did earlier? The way you were with him? Thank you, babe. Thank you. He needs it."

I shrug. I'm kicking myself for injecting this into our reunion when there's so much else I'd rather be talking about.

"Your dad will get there. He will. Eventually. I don't know if it helps you to know that, but it's true."

I shrug again. I totally feel thirteen again.

She takes my face in her hands once more. "Tyler, look at me." I do. "I'm sorry that you had to go through what you went through. It killed me to watch it all happening. Well, not exactly killed, but you know..." I smile, in spite of myself. "And it may not make any sense to you now, but everything that has happened to you happened exactly as it was supposed to."

"Really?"

She nods, gently.

"Well, that's fucked up."

"Fair enough. But there is another way to see it. And that's that it just *is*. And what you do with what *is* is what makes you *you*." She looks around again at our surroundings, "And baby, I'm so, so, so proud of who you've become."

My shoulders don't heave this time, and my breath doesn't quicken, but tears begin falling again. "You are?"

"Cross my heart," she says. And then adds, "I feel like I don't have to say the second part."

And just like that, Mom has me laughing again.

I don't care what she says. I have missed her so much. After I stop laughing, I take her hands in mine again.

"What now?"

"Sweetie..." Her shoulders rise and drop, and she lets out a sigh. "You know what now. She's waiting."

I look up at the sky, or whatever it is above us that seems bigger than sky. I look around at the water everywhere. The quiet, peaceful cataracts and the rippling, cresting waves. I notice the obelisks again and ask, "Do you know what those are holding up?"

She shakes her head. "Nope. But they look strong. Which is unsurprising."

"Why?"

"Because you built them."

And before another millisecond can pass, I have pulled us together and wrapped my mother in a hug. She hugs me back and strokes my head again.

"How can I bring you with me?" I ask, the sound of my voice muffled by her hair.

"The same way you keep me with you already," she says, softly.

I sniff through my tears so that I can say, "I love you."

She pulls back, looks me in the eyes – our eyes – and wraps her palms around my cheeks. "I love you, Tyler. More than you can ever know."

I slowly let my crying stop and then ask, "How do...?"

"Lie down here," she says, gesturing to the ankle-deep pool we're in. I do. The water splashes and laps around my ears.

"Now what?" I ask.

She steps back, away from me, and the water starts running by my ears faster. Louder. The pool is getting higher, engulfing me. Carrying me like I'm being run backwards down a water flume of some kind.

Over the increasingly noisy sound of the rushing river, I shout, "I love you, Mom!"

"I love you too, honey!" she calls out. And then, "Oh! Hey! Be careful!"

I smirk at that, because that's something she used to say when I was going off to do something dangerous. Which was all the time. And I offer the same response I used to give back then. "Come on, Mom. You know me. That's not gonna happen."

And she offers back the same retort she always used to give as well. "I know. But I have to say it anyway. I'm your mother!"

And then the current sweeps me away.

"One, two, three, four, five." I hear the count happening quickly and feel something heavy pressing on me. Then I feel something. Lips. Touching my lips. Perfect lips. Soft, delicate, kissable lips with a precious little Cupid's bow. Then again, I hear...

"One, two, three, four. Come on, you sorry son of a bitch!" And again, lips on my lips. And now I feel a pain in my chest. A weight. But a weight that feels like it's being lifted. No. Not lifted. Ripped. Ripped right out from the center of me.

And now I can hear coughing. And as I hear the coughing, I start to realize that it might be me who's doing it, because the sound seems to correspond with the searing pain I feel all through my ribcage and sternum. And now the coughing turns into gagging, and the gagging turns into something that sounds like vomiting, and then my eyes open and I can see a tiny geyser of water spurting up from my mouth.

And then a face enters my field of vision. Maddie's face. The look in her eyes is one of terror and astonishment. And even though I hate that part for her, I love that it's her I'm seeing. Because... because it's all worth it. Everything. Every cost, every loss, every moment that isn't absolutely perfect is made perfect just by virtue of her being.

And as I cough again, that pain is back, and I hear something that sounds like a crack. To be precise, it sounds like a bone cracking. To be even more precise, it sounds like a rib bone cracking. And to be very, very precise... It sounds like *my* rib bone cracking.

"Oh, shit!" I shout, as I roll over on my side onto the pool deck. Out of the corner of my eye I can see Logan's lifeless body floating in the water, a bloom of red expanding out away from him. And glancing down the length of me, I see a ripped t-shirt, soaked in my blood, tied around the place in my leg where the bullet went in.

"Ty? Ty? Tyler! Talk to me!"

"Hey, babe," I croak out. "Can you go back to the kissing stuff?"

"I wasn't kissing you! I was giving you mouth-to-mouth!"

"Oh. OK. Maybe I don't understand how kissing works."

She swings herself behind me and puts my head in her lap. Her naked lap. Where I am now looking up at her naked breasts, and just like that, Chuckie shows up to say hi.

She does kind of a double-take as she gives me a once-over and sees what's happening down below my waist. "Are you goddamn kidding me?" she says.

"I dunno, babe. It just happens. Cut me a break. I'm having a rough night."

"Christ. Can you stand up?"

"Maybe? I dunno. Do you need, like, all of your bones to stand up and shit?"

"OK," she says, rising up and laying my head gently down on the concrete. "Shit. I'm calling an ambulance. Stay here."

"May wanna call the cops too," I tell her as she's running inside. Watching her ass from my contorted position here on the deck makes me almost forget that I'm pretty fucked up. Almost. Then the pain shoots through me again and I'm reminded with a quickness.

"Damn. The cops. Yeah," she says. "What the hell will we say?"

"I dunno," I moan, my face now squarely against the ground. "Let's start with the truth and work our way backwards."

"Shit, shit, shit," she says, hopping from one foot to the next. "I don't wanna leave you here."

"It's OK. I ain't going nowhere." And then I moan again as the pain from kind of everywhere makes itself known. So this is what real, actual pain feels like. Yeah. This blows.

She comes running back over. "No, no way. I'm not leaving you."

"Babe," I say, summoning as much composure as I can. Which is actually just exhaustion, but it looks the same, probably. "Babe, I'm fine. OK? I'm fine. I'll be right here."

And now her lips start trembling. She nods, but the tremulous lips and scrunched-up face let me know that she's about to lose it. I work my way around to my back again, even though it hurts like a bitch, so that I can see her face. I take her hand and press it to my chest. My chest that is once again marked with the reminders of the life I've lived up to now. I don't mind that they're still here. They're part of me. They're part of everything I've been through. They're part of making me who I am. And that person is lying here holding Maddie Clayton's hand, so I must've done something right.

"Babe, listen. Grab the phone. I'm not going anywhere. OK? I will be here when you get back."

She sniffs back her tears, squeezes my hand tightly and says, "You will?"

"Where am I gonna go?"

"I dunno. You went somewhere a few minutes ago. I thought you were..." She chokes off before she gets out the last word.

"No way. I'm right here. Hey... I go where you go." I wink. Or blink. Not sure.

She sniffs one more time and says, "Promise?"

I think of all the things I could say. I could tell her that of course, I promise. I could tell her that I'll do my best. I could tell her that she has no idea what I would do to make sure that we're together for as long as possible. And even beyond that.

Yeah. I could say a lot of things.

But instead, I simply go with...

"Cross my heart."

I feel like I don't have to say the second part.

CHAPTER TWENTY

MADDIE

December 31ˢᵗ
New Year's Eve
11:50 PM

"Here. It's a regular-sized straw. I'll pour the juice
in a cup and you can drink it that way. OK? Please?" That's
me, talking to Tyler. The nurse gave up trying to get Tyler
to drink from the juice box – which he says he won't
because the tiny straw freaks him out – and went back to
the nurses' station mumbling something about "bullshit
way to spend New Year's Eve." But he has pills he's
supposed to take and he started choking when he
attempted to dry-swallow them, and then he spit them
back up.

I seriously don't think I could love him more if I tried.

The fact that he can be the toughest son of a bitch I
have ever met and the most hard-headed infant all at the
same time is just... well. It's perfect.

He tried to leave the ER last night and just go home,
but then he collapsed on his way out the door, so the
doctors insisted he be admitted. At least we were able to
get him a private room. I can't imagine we'd be here right
now if he had to share a room with somebody. I can't

imagine it because he said, "I ain't fuckin' staying if I gotta share a room."

The cops have been back a couple of times over the course of today. They actually just left a little while ago. We've now told them the whole story of exactly what happened three different times, but they just keep asking the same questions, always prefaced with some version of, "Let me make sure I'm getting this right."

We called Robert and Evan in Paris to kind of fill them in on everything that's happened. Evan wanted to jump on a plane and come straight back, but Tyler convinced him that there's nothing they can do, and we'll take care of stuff with the house. Although it's possible they won't be able to come home when they planned anyway, depending on how long their place is a crime scene. We had them on speaker and I did hear Robert saying in the background, "You didn't teach him how to turn on the alarm?" Which is a fair question and caused me to wonder how long Logan had been watching us in the house after we got back. But then that thought creeped me out and I decided it doesn't matter much now anyway.

We also gave the police Ricky's card to have them confirm everything we were telling them with him, but I don't know if they've been able to make contact. God only knows if Ricky's even still got a job. I hope he's OK. I wonder if we'll ever see that guy again. I dunno.

"I don't need no fuckin' pills," Tyler tells me now. "Seriously, babe. I'm fine. Know what? Let's get out of here. We've got ten minutes. We can get to the Strip and at least see some fireworks. K? Fun times. Let's go." He throws the sheets off his legs and goes for the IV drip in his arm, but I manage to stop him before he pulls it out.

"Will you stop?" I implore. "Babe, we're not leaving. Seriously. Give that up. We'll be able to see fireworks from the window. Here, I'll pull the shade up." I do.

"Fuck," he says, flopping back down. "I'm... Fuck. I'm sorry."

I sit on the edge of the bed and stroke his cheek. "Why? For what? What are you sorry about?"

He bites at the inside of his mouth and lets out a sigh. "We should be in a fuckin' treehouse and wearing loincloths and... I dunno. I'm sorry."

"Babe," I say, "I have no idea what the fuck you're talking about."

"Nothing," he mumbles. "Stupid."

I turn to him now and say, "Listen to me. OK? Please? Can you listen for a second?" His lips purse, like he wants to protest, but then he relaxes and nods.

And I begin.

"So... I used to think that there was a right way to do everything. It was what I would tell myself to excuse the fact that things seemed to be so off track for me. Like, I just hadn't figured out the right way yet, and the right way was out there and as soon as I could crack the code, everything would fall into place. You following me?"

He nods. I go on.

"And then you came back into my life, the way you did."

"I'm—"

"*And*," I cut him off, "I came back into yours. And, as we both well know, at that moment, it pretty much seemed like the worst thing that could have ever happened to me. In fact, I think I may have said words to that effect."

"Yeah, I may have heard something about it."

I kiss him on the forehead and go on. "But that's only because of the simple fact that I had an idea of what the right way to straighten shit out for myself might look like and it didn't, at all, resemble what was happening then. Right?"

"Sure."

"But this"—I gesture between the two of us—"this is, by far, and without even close competition, the best thing that's ever happened to me in my life. Do you get that?"

He shrugs and half mumbles, "I dunno."

"Well, if you don't know, then you're not paying attention. Because it is. You are. *We* are the best thing that's ever happened to *me*. And whether we're in some magnificent hotel suite somewhere, or on a beach in Mexico being shot at by drug runners, or in a hospital room on New Year's Eve, as long as it's *us*, I'm good, babe. As long as we're together, it *is* the right way for things to be. And I don't know if you can believe that, or if I could even explain why it's true, it just is. And so, while I now know that there isn't and never will be a right way to do everything, I know that as long as we're scaling Everest together, we'll figure out the best way to do it. For us. And we'll always reach the top. OK?"

There's a long moment of silence while he just stares at the wall, away from me.

"Babe?" I ask. "What is it?"

"That was just so beautiful that I don't wanna fuck it up by arguing that I would take the 'being shot at by drug runners' thing out of the speech, because that really did suck pretty bad."

I close my eyes, shake my head, and smile. "Just take your pills, dumbass." I stick the pills in his mouth and then place the straw to his lips as he sips.

Once he's finished swallowing, he leans back and lets his head land on the pillow. He grimaces a teeny bit. "You OK?" I ask. "Hurt too bad?"

"Nah," he says. "I think I'm just tired."

"Well, stay up for a couple more minutes so that I can kiss you at midnight while you're still awake, will ya?"

"Just a kiss?" he asks.

I look at him with arched eyebrows. "Why? What were you thinking?"

"I dunno." He shrugs. "That Chuckie should get to ring in the new year too."

I just start laughing, which I imagine I will be doing a lot of in the years to come, and I say, "You. Are. Insane."

"You're only just figuring that out?"

"No," I say. "No, it's been pretty obvious from the start."

"Yeah? And that doesn't freak you out? That you've hitched your wagon to an unpredictable maniac's train?"

I press my head to his so that I can look right into his eyes. "No," I say. "You wanna know why?"

He nods, and after I let out a small moan of want and desire and passion that lasts for several long moments, I tell him, with all the honesty that I feel in the depths of my once-filthy, currently being cleansed, evil, pure, devilish, angelic, and entirely contradictory soul that could never be satisfied with *anyone* more predictable...

"Because, Tyler Hudson Morgan, my love, there's no one else it could've been."

CHAPTER TWENTY-ONE

Silence. That's what I hear inside my head.
Silence.

Not one random thought. Not one errant notion.
Nothing. Nothing but the sound of Maddie's voice telling
me, in so many words, that she loves me.

I've been debating with myself whether or not to
share with her that I saw Scotty. And my mom. And Pete,
and Jeff, and Nadir, and...

But I don't think I will. Not now. Maybe someday.
But not just yet.

Not just yet.

*"There's no point in waiting to find Heaven. It's all already
there. You just have to seize it."*

*Yeah, Scotty. You're right. I get it, man. You're goddamn
right.*

And from somewhere down the hall, or from one of
the other rooms, I can hear the countdown beginning. *Ten,
nine...*

Maddie looks at me and smiles. *Eight, seven...*

I smile back at her so hard that it feels like my cheeks
will rip at the seams. *Six, five...*

She puts her lips right up against mine. *Four, three...*

And she whispers, "Happy New Year, Tyler Morgan." *Two, one!*

And when she kisses me, I whisper back, "Happy new everything, Madison Clayton."

She's right. I can see the fireworks from the window. Explosions. Tiny bombs going off in the night sky that signal new beginnings, and celebration, and hope. Distant and joyful eruptions of expectation and possibility.

And the very idea of that makes me laugh.

"What?" she asks, the smile still on her face. "What's funny?"

Glancing around at my broken and exhausted body, all strapped up to tubes and lying in this hospital room with Maddie here – multicolored rockets going off outside that seem to welcome the joyful coming of a new morning – I stroke her hair and tell her exactly what's so funny, remembering a thought I had not so very long ago...

"I just... I never dreamed Heaven would look like this."

END OF BOOK SHIT

JOHNATHAN

If you are reading this, the first thing I want to say is thank you.

Thank you for coming on this journey with us and immersing yourself in this adventure. I hope you have enjoyed it. (Presumably, if you've read all four books, then you have enjoyed it at least a bit — if you haven't enjoyed it, then you should take a look at why you want to punish yourself.)

I am a storyteller. All I want to do. And when Julie Ann Huss asked if I wanted to write romance novels with her, I saw it as an opportunity. I have devoted my life to the art (and the work) of both interpreting stories and creating ones I feel strongly about. There is a power in storytelling that I haven't found anywhere else, and I saw this as a different medium with which I could engage and share my love of the communal experience of discovered narrative.

When she and I began discussing what we would do and how we would introduce our collaboration, I asked Julie what she wanted out of partnering that would distinguish it from the work she had done on her own. She said a lot of things in response, but it can be distilled down to: She said she wanted to do something different, challenge herself, challenge the work, and stretch and grow via the process of writing with someone from outside her expected sphere. That sounded pretty good to me and I said, "great."

I then asked, "How far are you interested in stretching traditional boundaries?" She said, "Pretty far. What do you have in mind?"

So, what I'm going to talk about here is three things:

— What my goals have been (and continue to be) in writing books with JA Huss.

— What I wanted to achieve specifically with this particular book series.

— What it's like for me to be JA Huss's writing partner.

And I'm going to do that in reverse order.

BEING JULIE'S PARTNER

I would be hard pressed to identify a person I've met who suits me better as a creative collaborator than Julie Huss. If you read *Angels Fall* and that EOBS, then you already know that it isn't always smooth sailing. Julie and I can disagree a lot and sometimes vociferously. Once or twice they've even been the kind of disagreements that might've ended a less secure relationship. So, when I say that I know no one who suits me better as a partner, I'm not kidding.

But that doesn't imply that we share a brain, or the

same worldview, or even the same set of artistic or career priorities. It means that *despite* the ways in which we are different and the times when we disagree, we are able to move beyond – usually pretty quickly – the friction and get back to what's the most important thing to both of us: Making the best work we can.

That's only possible because we respect each other as people and we have an unceasing love and appreciation for the talent of the other. Only way it can work. There's no chance, if we didn't impress each other, that we'd even want to figure out how to navigate something as dense and complex as an effort like the one we're in together.

Respect is the centerpiece. And that's our anchor when seas get rough.

Julie recently described us as Kirk and Spock. I'm Kirk. She's Spock. I'm all passion, and emotion, and blood, and leap before I look. Julie's practical, and logical, and knows how to calculate the next best step. It may have something to do with the fact that I have no children, and Julie has done a spectacular job of raising two awesome humans to adulthood. There are things you learn from something like being a parent, and conversely there are risks you can afford to take when you're not accountable in that same way.

Maybe. Maybe not. But it's how we are.

Ironically, when it comes to the work itself, I tend to be the one who's methodical and deliberate and likes to plot and outline, and Julie's much more "write by the seat of her pants." Yet again, yin and yang. Fire and water. Kirk and Spock.

It is a credit to the balance in our dichotomy that when Julie asked what kind of thing I wanted to try writing first, and I said, "I'd like to do a multiple part exploration of the nature of self and love via a deep character study of the evolution of two wounded people, and also offer a commentary on mysticism and the salvation myth inside the framework of an extended allegory about loss and redemption," she didn't immediately hang up the phone.

The rest of the conversation was brief and went something like this:

Her: "So what you're saying is... You don't want to sell books."

Me: "What? No. Of course, I do."

Her: "Okay. But do you want to sell *these* books?"

Me: "Obviously."

Her: "So... For our first try, you don't wanna just write, like, kind of a fun, sexy book about hot people?"

Me: "... Why does what I'm saying and what you're saying have to be mutually exclusive?"

Her (god bless her): "...Yeah. I see that. Okay. Let's do it."

And that right there is why JA Huss is special.

She's not special because she's smart (although she is), and she's not special because she's a good writer (although I didn't set up a TV project at MGM television based on thirteen of her books because I don't already have enough to fill my days), and she's not even special because she has courage (although she does). Smart, talented, courageous people are actually probably about a-hundred-dollars a dozen (I don't want to make it sound *un*important – it's not common – it's just not as rare as people make it out to be).

What makes JA Huss special is that she has vision.

Vision is one of the rarest talents in this great universe.

And because of that vision, you are reading these

252

words right now. She knew that what we were going to undertake had the potential to be special in some way. And even if that specialness came with risks, she believed, with me, that the rewards would be worth it. And that doesn't mean writing an international bestseller, necessarily. It means laying a groundwork for a partnership that will show up to the party with a bang and grow stronger into the future.

Real talk? I am more demanding than you or anybody you know wants to deal with.

I mean, I'm one of the most delightful motherfuckers you'll ever meet, but I place an expectation of excellence on everyone around me. Because I never want to be the smartest person in the room. Whenever possible, I want to be learning from people who know more than I do. Or at least I want to be jockeying for a leadership role. I want to earn it. I want to fight for what's worth having. Julie and I push and activate each other in ways that are unique to anything I've known before.

And she will run the marathon to the last mile and never quit.

But at the same time ... she will allow me to steer when it's important.

And this is the part that speaks to a lack of ego I have only seen maybe a handful of times in my life.

So, after Julie said, "... Okay. Let's do it," we started plotting and writing. But partially owing to Julie's concurrent solo writing career and partially owing to something I'll talk about in a second, there came a point when I started requesting a little more.

Here's what I mean:

Again, we alluded to this a bit in the *Angels Fall* EOBS, but there would be times when I would have to assume some of the writing duties that were otherwise slated for Julie's computer. Workload was the thing that started it. Workload, time, hours in the day, etc. But as we got deeper into the series, I became very invested in the way things were going and began requesting if I could keep working even when it might be time to hand the work off to her.

And here is the part that is incomparable...

Julie would say, "...Okay." She would let me just keep writing. She would let me steer and maneuver. She trusted me to take things over and, *on OUR behalf*, move the tale along. And if you know anything about writers and writing and ego and being precious about work ...

I ain't never seen some shit like that in my life.

To be clear: We always still hand off to the other and if the other has notes, adjustments, revisions, etc., it's open season. The work is not proprietary to one of us. It is shared. It is not about her or me. It is what serves the book and tells the best story.

But as I became more and more passionate about things, Julie welcomed me to express *our* shared vision through *my* fingertips. And I'm honored.

For what we're doing, she is the best partner a person who is me could hope to have.

(**I'd like to offer one last comment about everything I just said:** Because of what I described, I would suggest that if you enjoyed these books, it is only because of our collaboration. And if there's stuff you *hated* about these books ... it's all my fault.)

WHAT I WANTED TO ACHIEVE WITH *THIS* SERIES

I wasn't joking about that thing I said to Julie. I wanted to get underneath the very DNA of romance and find a deeper meaning while exploring complex themes and universal truths.

Sounds pretty douchey.

Maybe it is.

But here's the thing: If someone asks you what these books are *about*, I want there to be an answer. In other words, I don't want you to say, "Oh, it's about Tyler and Maddie and blah, blah, blah, bullshit, bullshit, bullshit." That's the PLOT. Not what the books are ABOUT.

I have nothing against telling a good story. Quite the opposite. I think the only reason to tell a story is if you're aspiring to make it a good one. But I think there's a difference between a fun and entertaining story, and a *good* story. I hope, with these books, we have achieved both. I hope you have felt transported and diverted and entertained, and at the same time enriched and moved and stimulated to think about some things.

Moving forward, not every book that Julie and I write is going to be like this. But here. Now. These books... It was important to me that Julie and I SAY something.

One of the other reasons I wanted to work with Julie is that she doesn't write one thing over and over. That was very appealing to me. No person that I want to know is ONE thing. I don't know a rule that says an artist can only paint in one style, an actor can only play one kind of role, or a writer can only write one kind of book.

I also don't know of a rule that says a genre (like romance) can't reach beyond the genre and touch something else. What the hell is *Pride and Prejudice*, for crying out loud? Now, I'm not saying we wrote *Pride and Prejudice*. And if you say I did, I'll deny it and call you out as a liar. I'm pretty pretentious, but I'm not arrogant enough to believe that we made some kind of contribution to the literary canon that will alter the landscape of romance writing for eons to come. Or even for five minutes.

But I hope that if you hung in there with us, you got your arms around some of what we hoped to achieve and that your world feels just a little brighter for having taken the time to read. Hell, if all we did was offer you some escape for about 250,000 words, then that will feel very satisfying too.

MY BROADER GOALS IN WRITING BOOKS WITH JULIE

Kind of what I said above. It will depend. It will depend on the book, on the time, on the environment, on the subject, etc. I may just hope to make you laugh. I may just hope to make you cry. I may want to see if we can write a book where nobody calls each other by their name. I dunno. It will depend on what Julie and I decide together.

But I can say this, irrespective of other variables ...

I hope to discover things about the world while at the same time sharing a point of view that you'll not find elsewhere. I have always wanted to write a novel. And I never even thought of writing a romance novel. Which, when I stop to consider it, is odd for me. Because love, romance, passion ... These are the things I wake up for in the morning.

Love, in all its various permutations, drives everything I do. I feel deeply, and I hope to cause others to feel deeply as well. Feeling. It is the stuff of life itself. I strive to shine a light on the beating heart of our shared human experience whenever I can. It gives me a joy that I can't fully explain.

Again, if you're reading this, then you made it through. And together we have shared something special. I will never again write my first books. My first attempt at reaching readers and touching their hearts is over now. There will be other opportunities, and I'm sure the most aspirational and wide-reaching of chances to spread the stories of Huss/McClain (and at some point, I'm sure, of just Johnathan) are yet to be.

But this... This gift of perilous excitement and uncertain outcome that is *The Original Sin Series* by JA Huss and Johnathan McClain can never be replicated.

I'm privileged to have shared it with you. And I'm inspirited to see what happens next.

-JM
28 March 2018

OH! BONUS EOBS! THE <u>END</u> OF END OF BOOK SHIT, I GUESS!

I almost forgot. There are some little secrets and insider tidbits I thought it might be nice to share. There are many sprinkled throughout the books (if you were an existing JA Huss fan, the "Ford Aston" stuff in *Sin With Me* was for you, as you already know), but there are a few in this book specifically that nod to some things and I wanted to mention them to you.

MAROON 5

In Chapter 3, Tyler's dad asks if Tyler wants tickets to see Maroon 5 on New Year's Eve.

Maroon 5 does indeed play a New Year's Eve show

in Vegas at Mandalay Bay every year. My wife, Laura, and I happen to be friends with James Valentine, the lead guitarist for Maroon 5, and this past New Year's he gave us tickets to come see the show.

I also asked if he would hook Julie up and he did. So, Julie, Laura, and I all met up in Vegas to see the show and then we had pizza with James and his family afterward. So that reference is a little doff of the cap to that.

(PS: Those dudes put on one hell of a show. If you ever get a chance to check 'em out, go. Playing together in a band for a decade and a half makes you real, real good at your job.)

THE MANDARIN ORIENTAL

The Mandarin is the hotel we stay in when we go to Vegas. For two simple reasons.

— It's the only hotel on The Strip that is not attached to a casino (Technically the Four Seasons isn't either, but TFS is attached to Mandalay, which, as noted in this book, does have a casino), and when you're in The Mandarin it really is a spa-like escape.

— The Mandarin in Vegas is a *fraction* of the cost of a Mandarin anywhere else on the planet. Because even though there's no casino, they know that people ain't in Vegas for the seaweed body wrap. So, it's like, affordable. (Unless it's the holidays and you're staying in The Emperor Suite. Which we most decidedly aren't.)

I bring it up because when Julie, Laura, and I met over New Year's, Julie stayed at The Mandarin too. And we talked about these books. And we worked on these books. And it felt like a really important and special time.

THE SHOPS AT CRYSTALS

These are the boutiques across from The Mandarin, and I like shopping and don't really gamble. So, if I'm in Vegas for work, you'll know where to find me. And Julie insists on calling it "the mall." So that's where all the "mall" stuff in this book comes from. (After she read that I got a text from her saying, "It IS a mall!! LOL.")

Also, Julie and I sat in the Starbucks where Tyler and Maddie sit in this book, and just as they talk about their future, we talked about our writing future. The Asshole Mall.

87-3323

The short code number that Logan uses to text Tyler spells out "UR-DEAD" on the keypad.

I know. It's corny. But I like it.

FRANK'S

Frank's is not a real place. Frank's is a fictional place that exists in the Las Vegas of the television show CSI. I think it shows up maybe a dozen or so times over the course of the series.

The first episode in which the fictional Frank's appeared was called *Rashomama*. That episode of CSI premiered in 2006. And I was in it. I played the son of Ray Wise and Veronica Cartwright and it was my third television job in LA, and my first on a drama series. I also made one of my best friends shooting that episode and he is still one of my and Laura's closest mates to this very day. So. Frank's is an homage to that.

I GO WHERE YOU GO

Tyler and Maddie learn a lot in these books. And they do so quickly. Which is how life happens sometimes. You can't know a thing until you know it, and occasionally when you learn it, it's like the lights being turned on in a pitch-black room. It takes a moment for your eyes to adjust and for you to be able to comprehend what you're seeing. But then when you do, you can't believe that you didn't know it was there all along.

Theirs is a journey out of darkness into light. Out of pain and into comfort. Out of the blistering fires of torment and into the cooling waters of peace. They are both, in some ways, reborn. And part of that rebirth is informed by the new worldview they assume. A view of the world that causes a person to believe that the path to a full and complete life is one of generosity. Of giving. Of self-sacrifice. And that starts sometimes with looking at the person sitting next to you and committing to them in a full and total way.

Laura and I have been together about a dozen years now, married for almost eight. Early on in our relationship, for various reasons, we had to be on separate coasts a lot. I would fly back and forth from New York to LA, and she would do the same. Back and forth. A lot.

She was in a place where she was making some major life changes and I was deciding whether or not I would stay in LA and keep working in TV and film or whether I would go back to New York and do theatre. For a long time, neither of us were sure where we would land.

Eventually it became clear that I needed to be in LA. Had to be. Many reasons, but it was the choice I had to make.

Laura had pretty well settled on New York. She grew up there, it is home for her, and she loves it. It's where she's happiest.

And for a time, it appeared that ... that was it. We

weren't going to make it. It was going to be over for us.

And then, one day, she said, "I'm coming to LA. I'm moving there to be with you."

I was both elated and concerned. Because the last thing I *ever* want anyone to do is to make a sacrifice for *me*. It's just not something that makes me comfortable. Which is a whole other EOBS. But the point is, I was stunned. And after many, many, *many* hours of conversation and me asking, "are you sure?" over and over, I finally asked it one last time.

I said, "Are you **SURE**?"

And she looked at me, took a breath, and said, "I go where you go."

So. Here's the last thing I want to say ...

Everything I know about love... Everything I know about kindness... Everything I know about commitment, and dedication, and generosity, and sexiness, and passion...

In other words, everything I know that made it possible for me to write these books...

Hell, everything I know that makes it possible for me to wake up every morning excited and hopeful and ready to take on another day...

Everything that gives me the courage to keep climbing when I get tired...

All the art I create... All the music I hear... All the colors I see... All the joy I find...

Is because of her.

Laura, you are my heart, and I thank you for everything.

I have not the words to tell you how much I love you. But I hope you will accept all the words within the pages of these books as a woefully inadequate start. There will be many more.

I also hope you know...
I would walk through fire for you.
I would fight back the raging sea.
I will never flag.
I will never waver.
I will never not be there.
There is no measure of space or time that I would not cross to find you.
Always.
I go where you go.

JULIE

OK, my turn.

What a wild trip it's been these past 12 months. Today it's April 9, 2018 and it has almost been exactly one year since Johnathan and I started talking on the phone about our first collaborative project together (which was The Company pilot script). I remember that he and I were both in the middle of buying houses. Which is funny because we were commiserating on all kinds of shit that comes with house buying. He smashed his hand in a ladder while he was doing work on his house. That was the topic of one of our very first phone conversations. Thinking back on all that's happened in these twelve months I find it almost incredible.

We wrote a pilot script and made a deal with MGM, he came to visit me in Colorado, we wrote four books together, we met up in Vegas TWICE, and I went to LA to see him. Oh, and he narrated three audiobooks for me. Taking Turns (which was nominated for an Audie Award this year), Turning Back, and Anarchy Missing. And that doesn't even include all the projects we've done in our solo careers.

So we have been a couple of very busy motherfuckers.

And in between all that work, we had to forge a friendship as well. Which came pretty easy if you ask me.

Despite his admission that he is "more demanding than you or anybody you know wants to deal with" he is also incredibly easy to like. I don't know if it's because he's super funny, or he's a good storyteller (he can talk for hours!) or if it's because he's an actor, so everything that comes out of his mouth has a sort of dramatic flair that most people just don't have. I'd call him charismatic, but I have a personal dislike for that word. So I'll call him charming instead. He is utterly charming. Even when he's mad at me. lol I mean having arguments with Johnathan is like no other fight I've ever experiences. They are big, and loud, and colorful, and heated, and emotional, and then.... they are over. Like somehow we always come to a consensus (or maybe we tire ourselves out like children?) and things just... go on, ya know?

So we had this argument a few weeks ago. I honestly don't even remember what it was about. It was dumb, whatever it was. We were both tired, he was sick as a fucking dog, I was trying to finish up Pleasure of Panic and whatever... But it was all in email and let me tell you, we are writers, right? We can write some fucking emails. But the next time we talked he called me and I was in the car and he was all... "Uh... so..."

And I was all, "Fuck it. So we had a fight. Who cares? I got this new idea for a book. Let's talk about it."

And we did.

And I think that was the moment when I knew this was all real. Not the books, those are obviously real. But US. As partners.

So early on—this was like last fall—Johnathan gave me the title of a book to read about partnerships. It's called Powers of Two: Finding the Essence of Innovation in Creative Pairs. I listened to it on audiobook while I was in

Vegas. So I think of Vegas now when I think of that book. And this guy who wrote it, Joshua Wolf Shenk, is a friend of Johnathan's wife, Laura. And this was just after we finished The Company pilot script. I think we were in the pitching phase at this point. And we were already writing Sin With Me, but it was in the very early stages so all the stuff that comes from writing four books back to back hadn't come up yet.

And I loved that book. I loved hearing about how other people collaborate because this was my very first collaboration and I knew nothing about the process. We'd gotten through The Company script, which was very easy as far as my part went. Because he did almost all of it. I was more of a guiding force in that project.

And this Powers of Two book was really about figuring out one's role in a creative partnership. How you get inspired by each other, and bounce ideas off each other, and yes, argue and fight with each other so that what comes out of these messy conversations and feelings is something unique. Something only the two of you can do together. It's not me, it's not him, it's us.

And that's not something you can just decide, ya know? You can't just say, "OK, I'm in charge of this and your job is to do that." I don't think it works that way. It definitely didn't work that way for us and the reason that kind of division of labor stuff doesn't work in creative partnerships is because I think pain is part of the process. Which is ironic because I just wrote a book called the Pleasure of Panic. And there's a part of me that thinks I don't get pleasure out of things that come easy. It's the challenge I'm looking for. It's the angst of figuring things out. It's the panic when you fuck things up and have to try and fix it. It's the new idea that comes out at the end that makes you better than you were before.

I am definitely a better person today than I was last year and Johnathan **is** the reason why. Every conversation, every joke, every laugh, every fight, every email—all of it made me into Julie April, 9, 2018. And she's way more exciting. Way more knowledgeable. Way more open, and informed, and accepting than Julie April 9, 2017 was.

Being creative isn't easy—either alone or with a partner. You take ideas you have in your head. Ideas that come packaged up in emotions, and feelings, and the past—and you have to make that into something new. Something beautiful, but also sellable. And doing that alone is hard, yes. But doing that with someone else leaves you feeling incredibly exposed and vulnerable.

Because you have to discuss things. You have to get to the bottom of what meaning you're giving to these words.

Now... maybe what we did in this series isn't groundbreaking for anyone else but for the two of us—it is. It's raw, and it's real, and it's filled with feelings.

Not what YOU, the reader, are feeling.

But us, the writers.

We are in these pages. For better or worse, here we are.

And I couldn't be prouder of it.

The main theme running through these books, for me anyway, was that your past doesn't define you. That's the big one I was trying to get at. I kinda love this theme and if you've read my solo books then you know I hammer this one home a lot. And the reason I do that is because it's true as long as you believe it's true. And I know that there's lots of readers out there who read books to escape their real lives. It's a little vacation for them. A time when they don't have to worry about bills, or kids, or husbands, or housework, or jobs they hate and circumstances they can't control.

I know that. I know what these books mean to people.

I sell a fantasy life. But beyond that I sell an experience. A way for a reader to do things they'd never do, be places they'd never go, make decisions they'd never make, and then face the consequences of all those choices as one of my characters.

And now you get to do all that with one of OUR characters.

:)

When I started this whole collaboration thing I wanted to do it for my fans. I wanted to find new fans too, but mostly I wanted to give my current fans something more. Something brand new. Something exciting, and different, and cool. And Johnathan was—and still is—the perfect answer to what I was looking for.

I hope you fell in love with the journey of Tyler and Maddie. I hope you changed your mind back and forth about them several times before you landed on a decision. I hope the cliffhangers were the sweet kind and not the frustrating kind. I hope the end was what you were hoping for.

And I hope that you'll come back for more.

Because there's power in twos. And we've got more messy feelings to put on the page.

JA Huss
April 9, 2018

About the Authors

Johnathan McClain's career as a writer and actor spans 25 years and covers the worlds of theatre, film, and television. At the age of 21, Johnathan moved to Chicago where he wrote and began performing his critically acclaimed one-man show, Like It Is. The Chicago Reader proclaimed, "If we're ever to return to a day when theatre matters, we'll need a few hundred more artists with McClain's vision and courage." On the heels of its critical and commercial success, the show subsequently moved to New York where Johnathan was compared favorably to solo performance visionaries such as Eric Bogosian, John Leguizamo, and Anna Deavere Smith.

Johnathan lived for many years in New York, and his work there includes appearing Off-Broadway in the original cast of Jonathan Tolins' The Last Sunday In June at The Century Center, as well as at Lincoln Center Theatre and with the Lincoln Center Director's Lab. Around the country, he has been seen on stage at South Coast Repertory, The American Conservatory Theatre, Florida Stage, Paper Mill Playhouse, and the National Jewish Theatre. Los Angeles stage credits are numerous and include the LA Weekly Award nominated world premiere of Cold/Tender at The Theatre @ Boston Court and the LA Times' Critic's Choice production of The

Glass Menagerie at The Colony Theatre for which Johnathan received a Garland Award for his portrayal of Jim O'Connor.

On television, he appeared in a notable turn as Megan Draper's LA agent, Alan Silver, on the final season of AMC's critically acclaimed drama Mad Men, and as the lead of the TV Land comedy series, Retired at 35, starring alongside Hollywood icons George Segal and Jessica Walter. He has also had Series Regular roles on The Bad Girl's Guide starring Jenny McCarthy and Jessica Simpson's sitcom pilot for ABC. His additional television work includes recurring roles on the CBS drama SEAL TEAM and Fox's long-running 24, as well as appearances on Grey's Anatomy, NCIS: Los Angeles, Trial and Error, The Exorcist, Major Crimes, The Glades, Scoundrels, Medium, CSI, Law & Order: SVU, Without a Trace, CSI: Miami, and Happy Family with John Larroquette and Christine Baranski, amongst others. On film, he appeared in the Academy Award nominated Far from Heaven and several independent features.

As an audiobook narrator, he has recorded almost 100 titles. Favorites include the Audie Award winning Illuminae by Amie Kaufman and Jay Kristoff and The Last Days of Night, by Academy Winning Screenwriter Graham Moore (who is also Johnathan's close friend and occasional collaborator). As well as multiple titles by his dear friend and writing partner, JA Huss, with whom he is hard at work making the world a little more romantic.

He lives in Los Angeles with his wife Laura.

JA Huss never wanted to be a writer and she still dreams of that elusive career as an astronaut. She originally went to school to become an equine veterinarian but soon figured out they keep horrible hours and decided to go to grad school instead. That Ph.D wasn't all it was cracked up to be (and she really sucked at the whole scientist thing), so she dropped out and got a M.S. in forensic toxicology just to get the whole thing over with as soon as possible.

After graduation she got a job with the state of Colorado as their one and only hog farm inspector and spent her days wandering the Eastern Plains shooting the shit with farmers.

After a few years of that, she got bored. And since she was a homeschool mom and actually does love science, she decided to write science textbooks and make online classes for other homeschool moms.

She wrote more than two hundred of those workbooks and was the number one publisher at the online homeschool store many times, but eventually she covered every science topic she could think of and ran out of shit to say.

So in 2012 she decided to write fiction instead. That year she released her first three books and started a career that would make her a New York Times bestseller and land her on the USA Today Bestseller's List eighteen times in the next three years.

Her books have sold millions of copies all over the world, the audio version of her semi-autobiographical book, Eighteen, was nominated for an Audie award in 2016, and her audiobook Mr. Perfect was nominated for a Voice Arts Award in 2017.

Johnathan McClain is her first (and only) writing

partner and even though they are worlds apart in just about every way imaginable, it works.

She lives on a ranch in Central Colorado with her family.